Margaret Mayo

AT THE SPANIARD'S CONVENIENCE

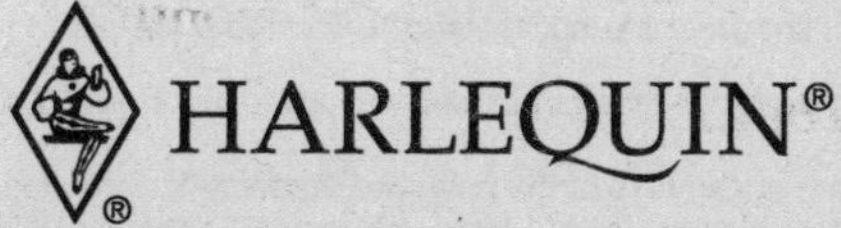

TORONTO • NEW YORK • LONDON
AMSTERDAM • PARIS • SYDNEY • HAMBURG
STOCKHOLM • ATHENS • TOKYO • MILAN • MADRID
PRAGUE • WARSAW • BUDAPEST • AUCKLAND

ISBN-13: 978-0-373-12602-6
ISBN-10: 0-373-12602-6

AT THE SPANIARD'S CONVENIENCE

First North American Publication 2007.

This edition published by arrangement with Harlequin Books S.A.

www.eHarlequin.com

Printed in U.S.A.

All about the author...
Margaret Mayo

MARGARET MAYO is a hopeless romantic who loves writing and falls in love with every one of her heroes. It was never her ambition to become an author, although she always loved reading, even to the extent of reading comics out loud to her twin brother when she was eight years old.

She was born in Staffordshire, England, and has lived in the same part of the country ever since. She left school to become a secretary, taking a break to have her two children, Adrian and Tina. Once they were at school she started back to work and planned to further her career by becoming a bilingual secretary. Unfortunately she couldn't speak any languages other than her native English, so she began evening classes. It was at this time that she got the idea for a romantic short story—Margaret, and her mother before her, had always read Harlequin romances, and to actually be writing one excited her beyond measure. She forgot the languages and now has over seventy novels to her credit.

Before she became a successful author, Margaret was extremely shy and found it difficult to talk to strangers. For research purposes she forced herself to speak to people from all walks of life and now says her shyness has gone forever—to a certain degree. She is still happier pouring her thoughts out on paper.

To my husband, Ken,
for all his love and support over the years.

CHAPTER ONE

KIRSTIE sat looking at the phone. She knew she had to make the call; she couldn't put it off any longer—she owed it to Becky. But it was the most difficult thing she had ever had to do. Fifteen years was a long time—almost sixteen actually. Would he even remember her?

She could remember Lucio Masterton as clearly as the day they had parted company. Black-haired, six feet four, disgustingly handsome, a powerful body—he'd played a lot of rugby in those days—and the most wicked sepia-coloured eyes she'd ever seen on a man. They could consume any member of the opposite sex with one glance, make her go weak at the knees and pray he'd take her to bed.

She had been the lucky one.

Or so she had thought!

It hadn't lasted. Lucio's sole interest in life had been becoming a millionaire. Bedding women came secondary. When she'd wanted to get serious he'd kicked her out of his life.

And now she needed to speak to him.

Now he was much more than a millionaire—he was a billionaire. A millionaire a million times over. The figures were incomprehensible.

But, to give him his due, his meteoric rise had been

achieved by hard work and not good luck. She had kept her eye on what he was doing over the years and despite her resentment over the way he had treated her she admired his tenacity.

According to the tabloids he was now one of the most eligible bachelors in Europe and was often seen with a good-looking woman on his arm, though none, so far, had become the much sought after Mrs Masterton.

Kirstie couldn't help wondering whether he treated them all with the same contempt with which he had treated her. The papers never gave reasons when he split with a girlfriend and, considering the fact that he'd now reached his pinnacle, Kirstie couldn't see the point in him remaining single. But would there ever be a woman good enough for him? Whom he wouldn't see as a threat to his way of life?

She lifted the receiver. It was now or never. And she dialled the number.

'LMT.' It was a singsong female voice that instantly grated on Kirstie's nerves.

'Can I speak to Lucio Masterton, please?'

'Who's calling?'

'Kirstie Rivers.'

'What company?'

'It's a personal call.'

'I'm sorry, Mr Masterton doesn't take personal calls, not unless they're on his approved list, and your name doesn't seem to be there.'

So he had a list of all his current girlfriends? Interesting.

'Very well,' she said, thinking quickly, 'it's Kirstie Rivers from Venture Applications.' Where that name had come from she had no idea but it seemed to do the trick.

'And what is the nature of your business?'

Kirstie couldn't believe she was being asked all these questions. 'What is this?' she asked angrily. 'The third degree? Lucio knows me. If you value your job tell him I'm on the phone.' Because there was definitely no way she could do this twice. It had taken enough courage this first time.

'Masterton.'

Oh, goodness, the girl had put her through without saying who she was. 'Lucio?' Horrifyingly her voice came out in a husky whisper.

'Who is this?' In contrast his voice was a rasp of impatience. A voice she remembered well. It was deep and gritty with a habit of vibrating along nerves and sinews, sending a tremor through every female who listened to it.

He'd had an air of authority, even as a young man of nineteen, but he'd honed his skills and it sat very well on his shoulders now, terrorising, she imagined, all who came into contact with him. Even his receptionist had had a healthy respect in her voice.

Kirstie cleared her throat, sat up that little bit straighter, stiffened her shoulders and spoke firmly. 'It's Kirstie Rivers.'

Silence!

Oh, lord! He *had* forgotten her. This wasn't going to be easy. She could picture the frown that drew his thick, shiny brows together; she could see his dark eyes narrowed and intent as he searched his memory, which, she imagined, would be encyclopaedic.

Should she enlighten him or wait and see what the search of his mind would throw up?

Ten, nine, eight, seven…

'Kirstie!'

He hadn't let her down. But was he smiling at the memory? Or was a frown etched into that dark Latin brow? He was a beautiful man. At nineteen he'd been handsome, and one of the most attractive boys in her college, but at thirty-four he was devastatingly magnificent.

Whenever his photograph appeared in a newspaper or magazine she studied it intently. Or when he was on TV talking about his latest project she listened to his deep, gravelly voice, feeling shivers of remembered passion run like wildfire through her veins. Crazy, she knew, but she couldn't help it. He had been her first love and her first lover. Not her only one—though there had not been many since—but none had matched up to Lucio Masterton.

'To what do I owe this pleasure?'

Pleasure! An unfortunate choice of word! Pleasure would be the last thing on his mind when he heard what she had to say. Kirstie's stomach curled into knots and her heartbeats quickened. Say what you've got to say and get it over with quickly, she told herself sternly. Otherwise you'll never do it.

How true that was. She'd put it off for years, but Becky had grown more and more insistent and so now was the time, her chance to—to what? To set the record straight. It sounded easy, but how would Lucio take it? She had no idea.

'How are you?' she asked.

'I'm quite sure you haven't phoned to discuss the state of my health,' he announced brusquely. 'I'm a very busy man, Kirstie, as you must appreciate. It's nice to hear from you but I'm due in a meeting in two minutes. Perhaps we could meet for a drink one evening and talk over old times. How about Thursday? I'm free then.'

'No!' Kirstie knew that if she didn't tell him now she never would. Her courage would desert her and she'd be letting her daughter down. Initially she had meant to suggest they meet up somewhere, but when push came to shove she couldn't do

it. She didn't want to see his face, to feel his anger first-hand. She wanted the safety of a phone line between them.

'What do you mean? No, not on Thursday? Or no, you don't want to meet me?'

'I mean I need to talk to you now.' Could he hear the crack in her voice, the dryness of her mouth? This was awful. No wonder she had put the moment off time and time again. 'You have a daughter, Lucio.' There, she had said it, not quite in the manner in which she had intended, but her secret was finally out.

Silence yet again!

Ten, nine, eight, seven, six, five…

Then the world exploded.

CHAPTER TWO

KIRSTIE felt sick with apprehension as they drew nearer to Lucio's house. It was at his insistence. He had not wanted to continue talking over the phone, nor even in a restaurant, but in his own home, where privacy was guaranteed. A home she was now seeing for the first time. A palatial mansion that screamed wealth!

Over the telephone earlier he had yelled so loudly that Kirstie had thought she would go deaf. Anger didn't even come into the equation. It had been more than that. It had been a red-hot fury that had sizzled along the line and set her phone on fire.

'I can't get out of this meeting,' he had snarled, when he finally seemed to accept that she was telling him the truth, 'but I can get out of a dinner engagement tonight. Be at my house at seven. I'll send a car.'

The line had gone dead.

Kirstie hadn't moved for at least ten minutes. She had expected anger and quick-fire questions, but she had not expected to have them thrown at her with the ferocity of machine-gun bullets. She had expected him to say it couldn't be true and for him to try and wriggle out of it. But he had not.

'I must see her,' he had declared.

'Not yet,' Kirstie countered fiercely. 'Becky doesn't know I've contacted you. We need to talk first. I don't want you frightening her.' He probably wouldn't—her daughter would probably be delighted to meet him at last—but she wasn't telling Lucio that, not yet anyway.

Having found the courage to tell Lucio the truth and having felt the full force of his fury, Kirstie was now dreading their forthcoming meeting.

Thankfully Becky was staying with a friend; she'd gone there straight from school, so there was no danger of Kirstie being questioned when the car came to pick her up.

A Bentley no less! She'd sunk into the rich leather upholstery and closed her eyes until they had pulled up outside Lucio's house, well-hidden from the road by dense woodland. Kirstie had no idea where they were. They could be one mile away or a hundred. Time hadn't mattered. She had lost herself in thoughts, in fear; in wishing she could turn back the clock.

Would Lucio have got where he was today if she'd turned up on his doorstep a couple of months after they'd broken up and told him that she was pregnant? Would he have married her and given up his big ideas? Or would he have accepted the inevitable but been an absentee father by still working all the hours God gave to build up a business? Or—the most terrifying thought of all—would he have turned her away?

She was greeted by, she presumed, Lucio's butler, a grey-haired, erect man in his mid-fifties with a kindly face. 'Come this way,' he said, and she followed him to a room at the back of the house overlooking formal gardens. It was a huge room, as she guessed they all were in this massive house, and she looked about her with interest. It told her nothing about Lucio. It was as impersonal as a room could get. How could he be happy living in such a soulless place?

She stood at the window and didn't hear Lucio approach, jumping suddenly at the sound of his voice. 'Why don't you sit down?'

Kirstie turned and for the first time in nearly sixteen years looked into a pair of sepia eyes that had once had the power to send her whole body into a state of desire so strong it filled every limb and every nerve and tissue. She had expected the feeling to have died long ago. Instead a shock wave ripped through her.

He still had the power!

Her whole body reacted violently and it took every ounce of her strength to slam the sensation back down to where it belonged. This man was no longer for her. He had hurt her incredibly. She ought to hate him. He had ruined her life, or so she had thought at the time. In fact, Becky had been a blessing. So what, then, was this feeling? Desire for a good-looking, sexy man? Lust even? But certainly nothing more!

Her legs felt weak and, although she didn't want to sit, she moved towards an over-stuffed red velvet chaise longue and perched herself on the edge of it, her amethyst eyes huge as she looked up into his face. But when Lucio didn't take a seat, when he continued to look at her with a frown so deep on his brow that it threatened to slice it in two, she jumped up again.

'Say what you've got to say and let's get it over with,' she heard herself mutter. This was nothing like the conversation she had intended to have with him. She had planned to be reasonable and unruffled; to let him see that what had happened was no fault of hers.

He put his hand on her shoulder and forced her to sit again, and then he stood over her like Goliath over David. The heat from his hand remained even when he had removed it, a telling reminder that if he so desired he could persecute her with ease.

'Why did you never tell me I had a daughter? In fact, why did you never let me know that you were pregnant?' His almost black eyes bored into her soul like laser beams, pinning her even more firmly to her seat. 'And more to the point, why have you decided to tell me now? Is it because you need money?' he asked scornfully. 'Fifteen-year-olds take some keeping, so I understand, and then there'll be university fees and all it entails, and—'

'It's not about money,' Kirstie cut in furiously. 'How dare you insinuate that that's what I want?'

'Then pray tell me,' he rasped, his face a mask of ice and fury, 'exactly why you've chosen this moment to tell me I have a daughter. Providing, of course, that she *is* my daughter.'

Kirstie gasped. 'Do you really think that I would lie to you?'

'There are women who would, if they thought they'd get something out of it.'

'I want nothing from you,' she snapped, her heart beating so furiously that she could hear its echo in her ears. It was like a drumbeat that threatened to drive her mad. How could he think that she would be so coldly calculating? Hadn't their months spent together taught him anything about her?

He stood tall and proud in front of her, his arms folded over his magnificent chest, his feet apart, reminding her of a king, autocratic and regal. And Lucio was just as outstanding. He probably thought of himself as the royal head of his business empire.

'So, the question remains, why are you telling me now?'

He sounded as though he wasn't even remotely interested in the fact that he had a daughter. The very thought of it made Kirstie's blood boil and she snapped her question at him. 'Don't you want to know about her? Don't you want to know her name? What she looks like? Whether she's like you, in fact?' Which she was, very much so!

She had the same-shaped eyes, the same colour even, although maybe Becky's were a touch lighter. The same straight nose; even their mouths were similar. There was no mistaking that she was Lucio's daughter and he would see that for himself when…

Kirstie stopped her thoughts there. Steady on, she told herself. Lucio wasn't showing much interest in Becky. He was more concerned with what *she* might be trying to get out of him.

'Of course I want to hear about her,' he snapped derisively, 'but I need to be sure first that she is my daughter. Any self-respecting mother would have chased up the father long before now. She'd have been banging on his door the moment she discovered that she was pregnant. Why weren't you?'

A flash of contempt deepened Kirstie's eyes into the darkest of purples. 'You really think I'd have done that after the way you cast me out of your life?'

'I did not cast you out, as you so *delicately* put it,' he roared. 'You were the one who did the walking. I had no time for marriage and you knew it.'

'But you had time to use my body,' she thrust back fiercely. Lord, the arrogance of the man. Nothing was his fault!

'From what I remember, you were as willing as I.' Dark eyes were fierce on her face, daring her to refute it.

Of course, he must know that she couldn't. They had been insatiable. They had spent almost all of their free time together in bed. Her cheeks flushed hotly at the very thought. She'd felt no shame; she had been confident in Lucio's love for her. Until he had thrown it back in her face! 'I was willing, yes, because I thought you loved me,' she flared. 'I didn't realise that you were more in love with the idea of making millions. I really couldn't compete, could I? But you left me one lasting legacy.'

'Which you didn't even have the decency to tell me about,' he spat icily. 'And I still don't know that you aren't trying to trick me.'

Kirstie snatched up her bag from the floor where she had dropped it and, taking out a photo, thrust it into Lucio's face. 'Tell me now that you don't think she's your daughter.'

He studied it for so long without speaking that Kirstie began to feel irritated. 'What's wrong? Can't you see the likeness?'

Lucio's nostrils flared and his eyes were as hard as bullets when he finally looked at her again. 'My guess is that you've been telling my daughter lies about me.'

'What?' she gasped. 'Why would I do that?' And it was *my* daughter now, was it? He'd accepted that she was telling the truth.

'You tell me. Has she never asked about me? I can't believe she hasn't wanted to find her own father.'

'Of course she's asked.' Kirstie's eyes flared hotly. 'But do you really think I would have told her that her father was more interested in making money than parenthood? What sort of a complex do you think that would have given her?'

His face hardened even more until it looked like carven stone. 'You don't know that for a fact.'

'No?' she scorned. 'Tell me, what would you have said if I'd turned up on your doorstep claiming I was pregnant?'

He didn't answer; he simply looked at the photograph again. 'So what have you told her about me?' he asked more quietly.

'Nothing much! I told her I once loved you; I didn't want her to think that I'd slept with you for the sheer hell of it. But I also told her that I no longer knew where you lived.'

'But you could have found me, like you have now.' Hard eyes bored into hers.

'I could have.'

'So why didn't you?'

Kirstie glared at him, her eyes full of fire. 'For one thing I wasn't sure you'd want to know about her. I'd already proved to be a nuisance in your life; what would you have said if two of us turned up on your doorstep? You'd blame me for getting pregnant—it would have had nothing to do with you,' she added derisively, ignoring his sudden harsh frown. 'You'd have claimed I was ruining your plans. You might even have said that I'd done it on purpose so that you'd have to marry me. You see, Lucio, I found out that I didn't know you at all. And I didn't want to take the risk of being rejected for a second time.'

Lucio went very quiet, simply standing watching her through narrowed eyes until she could take it no more. With a shake of her head Kirstie got to her feet and would have walked out the door if he hadn't caught her arm and spun her to face him.

It was the first time in over fifteen years that she had stood close to him, so close that she could smell the clean freshness of him, and a very faint whiff of something exotic. Sandalwood perhaps, musk, spice! Something intoxicating and dangerous!

'Don't you dare run away after the bombshell you've just dropped,' he hissed through gritted teeth. 'I cannot turn back the years, as you are well aware, but I can hopefully make up for lost time. I want to meet my daughter. And I think now would be a very good time. I'll drive you back to your house and—'

'No!'

Lucio frowned, a deep, dark frown that sent savage lines radiating over his forehead, and long, strong fingers gripped her shoulders hard. 'What do you mean, no?'

'I mean that Becky's not home. She's sleeping at a friend's tonight.'

* * *

Lucio found it hard to believe that Kirstie had chosen to keep his daughter a secret for so long. And it was even more puzzling that she had chosen now to tell him. Why? Why after fifteen years? Why not after one, two, or even three? Why at all? What had finally pressured her into seeking him out?

With one short phone call she had turned his life upside down. He had achieved his life's ambition. The success of his IT company was even more phenomenal than he'd ever imagined. And he'd done it all on his own. He had no partners; he'd gone every step of the way himself. He'd taken over companies, he'd made enemies, but he also had good friends. He was respected in the industry worldwide. He had a good life. And now Kirstie had thrown it into turmoil.

This was far worse than any work problems he'd ever encountered. He had a daughter! And she was fifteen years old. *Fifteen!* He'd missed out on the best part of her life. He'd not heard her first word. He'd not seen her take her first step. He'd not heard her call him Daddy.

He closed his eyes, let Kirstie go, and his heart felt heavy in his chest. What had she done to him? He was aware that he'd hurt her when he said he didn't want to get married, but surely she must have known that he wouldn't have turned her away if she'd told him that she was carrying his child? This was the hardest pill to swallow.

He wanted to see his daughter. *He wanted to see her now!* He would never catch up on the missed years but there was so much he could offer her, so much he could give her.

He'd known instantly from the photograph that she was his. It was like looking at an old photograph he had seen of his mother when she had been Becky's age. The girl had the same dark hair, the same smile, the same everything. He wondered what Becky was short for. Probably Rebecca, which actually he preferred! It sounded more dignified, more grown up. Becky would have been a perfectly suitable name when she was a child, but he hadn't been a part of her life then. Now he felt she needed a name to suit their new life together, something more mature. His daughter would from now on be known as Rebecca.

'So when can I see her?' he asked with some irritation. Why on earth had Kirstie chosen to tell him about his daughter at a time when she wasn't around?

'I don't know,' answered Kirstie, her eyes stone cold on his. 'I've not even told Becky that I was coming to speak to you.'

Lucio frowned. Had she been afraid that he wouldn't want to know? Had she thought that he'd turn Rebecca away the same as he had her all those years ago? He'd had his reasons then but he wouldn't do it now, especially not to his own flesh and blood. Was that what had stopped Kirstie? Was she bending to pressure from her daughter? If so it must have cost Kirstie a lot of courage to phone him this morning.

And now? The bombshell had been dropped but he was glad that it had. It was time he settled down and looked after his personal life instead of his business and his hundreds of employees. It was hard running a worldwide business single-handed; time perhaps to delegate, something he had always railed against.

He had managers naturally, hand-picked men whom he could trust, but he always insisted on making final decisions himself. His business didn't even involve a lot of international travel these days. With the high technology they designed and used he was able to keep his finger on every pulse right from his London office. He had a room with a bank of screens where he could talk to any single employee in any country of the world face to face.

'Correct me if I'm wrong, but wasn't she the one who wanted to meet me?'

'She does,' answered Kirstie. 'But I wanted to speak to you first, make sure that she'd be welcome in your life.'

'You doubted it?' A fearsome rage consumed him. 'You doubted that I'd acknowledge my own daughter? What sort of a monster do you take me for?' He didn't wait for her answer. 'Where is she, Kirstie? I want you to fetch her, right now!'

But Kirstie shook her head. 'She needs to be told in my own time. I refuse to rush this. I'll be in touch with you again in a few days. Shall I ring your office or here?'

Lucio stared at her. A few days! She was going to leave him in limbo for a few days! The hell she wasn't. 'I won't wait that long,' he roared. 'Tomorrow! You will bring her here tomorrow evening and that is final!'

CHAPTER THREE

KIRSTIE spent the whole day wondering what would be the best way to tell her daughter that she had finally traced the man who had fathered her and, more importantly, that she was going to meet him that very evening.

Any minute Becky was due in from school and Kirstie's heart thumped unsteadily. She'd done nothing all day, leaving her very able assistant to run things for her, telling him that she had a migraine and was staying in her darkened bedroom.

She ran a software business from home; it was the only way she'd been able to work and look after Becky at the same time. And it was doing very nicely. But today she'd given it no thought at all. Her mind was in turmoil.

There was no doubt that Becky would be excited and eager to meet the father she knew nothing about. But Kirstie was worried. Lucio was so rich and powerful that she was afraid he might try to buy Becky's love with gifts. He wouldn't give up his time for her, she felt sure. Maybe in the beginning, but then he would go back to making money. Money was his god, his slave, his everything.

Admittedly he gave money to charity; she'd read that in the papers, and he was always quoted as being a very generous man. But he could afford it. It wasn't like giving your last penny to a hungry child. It didn't leave him short. It probably helped him with his tax bill if the truth were known.

Realising that her bitterness wouldn't help Becky, Kirstie tried desperately to calm her troubled thoughts. This would be a happy day for her daughter; she needed to be happy too. She took a shower, brushed her shoulder-length auburn hair until it shone, pulled on a soft crêpe sage-green suit and then fixed a smile on her lips.

When her daughter came in she knew nothing of her mother's inner turmoil. 'You look nice, Mum. Are you going somewhere?'

Kirstie hugged her daughter. 'We're both going out, later, but first of all there's something I have to tell you.'

There were tears in Becky's eyes when Kirstie had finished. 'I'm actually going to meet my father at last? Tell me what he's like, tell me all about him.'

But Kirstie hadn't much to tell. After all, she'd only known him for a few short months. He was a very different man now. If she had thought him a mature teenager he was an even more devastating man. In fact, she would go so far as to say that she had never seen a better-looking male. It was no wonder he was never short of girlfriends.

She couldn't help wondering why he had never married. Perhaps he'd realised that they were all hangers-on, that none of them loved him for himself. And she could understand why. He gave the impression that money meant more to him than anything else in the whole wide world. He would wine them and dine them, buy them trinkets and take them to bed. But it wouldn't be love that he felt. In actual fact he led rather a sad life. She didn't feel sorry for him, though; he had brought it all on himself.

When Lucio's Bentley arrived complete with liveried

driver Becky was duly impressed. 'Wow, Mum, he must be very rich. Wait till I tell the girls at school about this.'

And wait until you see his house, thought Kirstie.

Becky was actually speechless when they drove along the tree-lined drive and the mansion came into view. Her jaw dropped to her chest, and when the butler led them inside her eyes were as wide as saucers.

They were shown into the same impersonal room as yesterday and Kirstie's fury knew no bounds when Lucio kept them waiting for several minutes. He had been so eager to meet his daughter and yet he couldn't be there to greet them. Not that Becky seemed to mind; she skipped around the room, looking and touching and exclaiming, and her face was so excited that Kirstie couldn't remain angry.

'My father owns all this?' she asked in a hushed whisper.

'I do.'

Neither of them had heard him come into the room and Kirstie whirled. He had eyes only for Becky. And she him! The likeness between them was unreal. It was no wonder she had never forgotten him. She'd had a constant reminder all these years.

From somewhere she found her voice. 'Lucio, this is Becky.'

'Becky—' she looked at her daughter, her eyes suddenly full of tears '—meet your father.'

As still as a statue now, Becky looked at him with wide, enquiring eyes. And for once she was silent.

In fact they both seemed tongue-tied, simply looking at each other for long, aching seconds, wondering why they had only just met, why all those years had gone by without either of them knowing about the other. Kirstie's heart ached too. Because it was her fault.

She realised in that instant that she had done her daughter

a disservice. Lucio too, but he was old enough to take things in his stride. Becky was at her most impressionable age. Teenage years were bad enough without this. Kirstie hoped and prayed that all would go well, that Lucio wouldn't let her down. Becky had so much wanted a father, her real father. It was her dream come true. But would Lucio live up to it?

'Rebecca.'

Kirstie frowned. Rebecca! Where had that come from? No one ever called her daughter that. In fact, Becky hated it.

And he opened his arms.

Kirstie held her breath.

An age went by, and then slowly, cautiously, questioningly, her eyes never leaving those of the man who was her father, Becky walked into them.

A huge lump filled Kirstie's throat. It was a moment she had never thought would happen. She had imagined, if they ever did meet, that there would be an awkwardness between them. Instead Becky seemed more than ready to accept her father. Perhaps because she had so yearned to meet him.

Lucio's arms folded around her and his eyes closed—this was clearly an emotional moment for him too. And when he let her go Kirstie saw him quickly blink away tears.

'Welcome into my life,' he said quietly. 'We need time alone, Rebecca. We need to get to know each other. How would you like to come to my home in Spain for your school holidays?'

Kirstie felt an immediate panic, but the girl's eyes widened with delight and she looked enquiringly at her mother and then back to the father she had just met. She had instantly and unreservedly taken to him, thought Kirstie. It was crazy; it was unbelievable! Or was it?

Becky had known her mother must trust him or she would

never have arranged this meeting. But had his obvious wealth gone to her head? Would she have taken to him so immediately if he'd been a poor man? Was she looking at the wider picture and imagining what he could give her? Kirstie realised she needed to have a good talk with her daughter before any decisions were made.

'I think it's too soon to even think about anything like that,' she said sharply.

Lucio frowned.

Her daughter pouted.

But Kirstie was adamant.

'It seems to me, Rebecca, that your mother and I have a few things to discuss,' Lucio said. 'How would you like to go and explore the house?'

'May I?' asked Becky, wide-eyed. 'Can I go anywhere?'

'You may, but don't touch my computers.'

'I won't, I promise. This is great, Mum.' And with her eyes shining like Christmas-tree baubles Becky danced from the room.

'How dare you suggest taking Becky away from me?' Kirstie raged at once.

'I'm not going to take her away from you. I just think we—'

'That's the trouble, you're not thinking,' she declared fiercely. 'Becky doesn't know you. She's impressed by what you represent, but she needs love too. She needs loving, caring parents and you'll never be that. Having Becky live with you will be a five-minute wonder. She's not going anywhere with you.'

'You'd deny me the pleasure of getting to know my own daughter?' A slow rage began to fill his face, dark anger that made Kirstie's stomach muscles tighten.

'Yes!' If he was taking her to Spain!

'You've had her for fifteen years and yet I can't have a few weeks on my own with her?'

'You don't even know her yet, nor does Becky know you. I'm not having you take her to some foreign country where I won't even be able to see her. You can get to know her just as well here. Or would you be too busy for that?' she thrust derisively, at the same time unable to ignore an unwanted *frisson* of awareness that had unnervingly made itself felt.

'We both know,' she went on, 'how many hours you put in at work. The poor girl will soon realise that you're not the golden idol she thinks you are. She's impressed by all this, but believe me—'

'Enough!' Black eyes glittered. 'I am going to get to know my daughter, believe *me*. You've done enough harm already.'

'Harm?' she queried angrily.

'By keeping her from me! The school year ends in a few days. Rebecca is off for six weeks. I want her to come to Spain with me.'

So he had done his homework! 'You don't care that we might have plans?'

'Have you?'

Kirstie shrugged. 'Actually, no!' Becky no longer wanted to go on holiday with her; she wanted to go with her friends instead. They'd had a huge row over it only the other day because Kirstie didn't consider her daughter old enough to go away without parental control.

'Then I don't see what the problem is.' His eyes had gentled, as though he was thinking along the lines that persuasion might be better than demands. 'Unless of course you're thinking that I might kidnap my own daughter and you'd never see her again?'

Such a thought had never occurred to Kirstie but now her head jerked. 'Would you?' And her blood ran cold.

'Of course not! What do you take me for?' He closed the space between them and ran the back of a gentle finger down her cheek. 'I want what is best for both of us. Though if you intend to be awkward…' There was a veiled threat behind his words. 'I need to get to know my daughter. Surely you understand that?'

Kirstie nodded, trying to ignore the tremor his touch had created. It curled around her heart and resurrected memories she would rather forget. 'I want what is best for Becky,' she said tersely. 'She's excited about meeting you but I refuse to let her join you in Spain—unless I come too.'

Lord, that was the last thing she wanted but she'd said it now. He could take it or leave it. It was the two of them or neither of them.

Lucio smiled. 'You'll be very welcome.'

Kirstie had stunned him by her suggestion. He had thought he'd have a much bigger fight on his hands where Rebecca was concerned, and he didn't mind at all if her mother joined them.

What an insatiable lover Kirstie had been. A little too possessive in the end, but quite an animal in bed! His blood ran liquid and hot through his veins as memories came tumbling back. He'd had his regrets, he'd had them in plenty, but always he'd thrust them firmly from his mind, concentrating instead on building up his business.

When they met yesterday he had been totally unprepared for the swift echo of feelings that rose inside him, and if she was going to join him in Spain…

He'd had relationships since, naturally, but no one had thrilled him the way Kirstie had, and still did! He'd have to be careful, or he'd frighten her away before she even joined him.

'I'll make the arrangements,' he said, careful to keep his

tone neutral. If she even guessed at the thoughts racing through his mind she would run a mile. She'd made it exceedingly clear that she had no time for him. What she was doing was for her daughter alone.

'Then we'll go,' she said, backing away.

'You don't want the grand tour yourself?' It was meant as a joke but he saw the distaste in her eyes and it saddened him. He was proud of his achievement and he'd have liked Kirstie to have found pleasure in it too.

'Becky!' Kirstie stood at the bottom of the grand curved staircase and looked up. 'Becky, I'm ready to go.' She hated this house; it didn't impress her one bit. She was doing all right for herself these days, and had a nice house too, but this was way over the top.

'Are you happy in a place like this, Lucio?' she couldn't help asking.

He frowned. 'Why shouldn't I be?'

Kirstie shrugged. 'It's very grand, for a man on his own. Or am I wrong in assuming that? Is there a Mrs Masterton these days?' She knew there wasn't, she had read it in the papers, but she didn't want him to know that she eagerly scoured everything that was written about him.

'No, there's—no one.'

She noticed that he seemed to hesitate and guessed that there was someone in the offing but he didn't want to talk about her. 'So why such a huge house?'

'Because I do a lot of corporate entertaining. I've come a long way, Kirstie, since you knew me. A lot of deals have been finalised here. I have no regrets about owning such a place. I'm sorry you don't like it.'

'I didn't say that.'

'But you don't, do you?'

'It's not to my taste, that's all.'

'So what is your taste? Maybe I'll drive you home myself and find out. Ah, here's Rebecca.'

'Mum, you should see the ballroom. You could have fabulous discos there.'

'And so you shall,' said Lucio with a smile that revealed his perfectly even white teeth. 'You can celebrate your sixteenth birthday here. You can invite as many friends as you like and—'

'I think not,' cut in Kirstie firmly. 'You're not buying your daughter's friendship, Lucio. I absolutely forbid it. Come on, Becky, let's go.'

She went out through the tall doors in a fury, Becky running to catch her up. The Bentley sat on the drive, waiting. Kirstie opened the back door and slid in before Lucio could even think about helping her.

'Can I sit in the front?' asked Becky eagerly.

'Of course,' said Lucio.

'Certainly not,' answered Kirstie, and then brought herself up with a jerk. She didn't want Becky being caught in the middle of their hostilities. The girl was thrilled at finding her father and needed to spend time getting to know him. 'I'm sorry,' she corrected. 'Of course you can.'

The car was sumptuous and spacious and Kirstie felt a million miles away from them. She couldn't even hear what they were saying so she sank back into her seat and closed her eyes. She was not looking forward to inviting Lucio into her home, but she knew that she'd have to. It was natural that he'd want to see where his daughter lived.

The journey took no time at all and when they got there Becky said, 'Mum, can Dad come in?'

It was the way Becky said Dad so naturally that got to Kirstie. Her eyes caught Lucio's in the mirror and she knew that she dared not deny his daughter this pleasure.

Her house wasn't small but somehow Lucio managed to fill it with his presence. The moment he entered it the air thickened around her and she found it difficult to breathe. It was a relief when Becky took him upstairs to show him her room with her computer and disco lights. But all too soon he came down again and amazingly he seemed completely at home.

She could remember his student flat that he'd shared with another guy. It had been the pits but it hadn't seemed to bother him. And now he was equally happy here in her kitchen as he was in his own grand palace.

'You have a nice house,' he acknowledged.

Kirstie hadn't shown him around; he didn't know that she had an office suite at the side, and she didn't really want him to know yet that she ran a successful company. Or that she'd even had dealings with his firm! Not yet anyway. This was all about their daughter; she didn't want to mix the two. Time enough to tell him when he asked what she'd been doing all these years.

'I like it,' she said. 'And Becky's happy here. Her friends all live close; they pop in and out all the time. It's good.' And she wanted him to know that she wouldn't approve if he tried to tempt her away.

'I guess I should be leaving,' he said finally, and Kirstie was relieved. 'Where's Rebecca?'

'On her computer, I imagine. Emailing or chatting with her friends, telling them what a fab new dad she has.'

Lucio looked pleased. 'I'm glad she liked me. She's a lovely girl and a credit to you.'

He drew close and Kirstie was afraid that he was going to

kiss her. Her heart changed into rapid overdrive and her pulses went wild. And when his mouth came down on hers she knew that nothing had changed.

CHAPTER FOUR

THE kiss lasted for no more than a few seconds, but in that brief space of time it resurrected everything Kirstie had ever felt for Lucio, and alarmed her so much that she backed away furiously. 'How dare you?' She almost slapped his face and then thought better of it.

How could this happen after all these years? Hadn't she learned anything? Lucio wasn't into relationships; he was a playboy. He would play with her feelings and then leave her high and dry. Again.

Glaring at him fiercely, she couldn't help noticing a sprinkling of grey hairs at his temples, and a few lines carved into his face where there had been none before. Long hours spent working taking its toll? Long, sleepless nights with a pretty woman in his bed? Or simply the normal ageing process that had turned him into hot property? Amazingly, though, she had an insane urge to run her fingertips along each one of those age lines. Maybe even her tongue!

Then anger took over. How could she feel anything for this man? He was formidably sexy and unfortunately could still arouse her by just looking at her, but she had to find the strength to resist him, show him that he no longer meant anything to her; that he was out of her system for good. He might be the father of her child but that was as far as it went.

A faint, cynical smile turned up one corner of his beautifully moulded lips, annoying her even further.

'If you think that we can take up again where we left off then your conceit has got the better of you,' she exploded, hoping fervently that he hadn't felt her response.

It hurt that Lucio should think she was good enough for one thing only, and if it wasn't for her daughter she would have ordered him out of her house and told him she never wanted to see him again. But she knew in her heart of hearts that she couldn't let Becky down. Kirstie had never seen her so excited. Becky was so much looking forward to getting to know her father, and a holiday in Spain was the icing on the cake as far as she was concerned.

'I wouldn't even think of it,' he rasped. 'You've deprived me of seeing my daughter grow up; how do you think that makes me feel about you? It was a goodbye kiss, that's all, the same as I would give my mother.'

Kirstie didn't believe him. His mother indeed! He'd been testing her, and heaven help her if she'd given herself away. The last thing she wanted was for him to know that just one look at the long, hard lines of his body was enough to send her emotions into overdrive.

Tossing her hair back from her face, she marched from the kitchen to the hallway and swung open the front door.

Annoyingly he made no effort to walk through it. 'I'd like to say goodbye to my daughter first.'

Kirstie glared at him, not wanting to prolong this moment a second longer than she had to. 'Becky,' she called, 'your father's leaving.'

The girl galloped downstairs and, much to Kirstie's annoyance, threw herself into Lucio's arms. Did she have to be so overwhelmingly pleased to have met him? Kirstie questioned angrily. Why couldn't Becky have been shy and faintly scared, reserving her judgement until she got to know him better? This all-out show of love and affection worried her.

After Becky had returned to her room Lucio's face changed from one of soft indulgence to a hard mask of indifference. 'I leave for Spain in the morning. I'm spending time at my office there. You'll be hearing from me regarding your travel arrangements.'

He made it sound like a business deal and Kirstie's hackles rose. But she thought of her daughter upstairs, and her excitement at finally meeting her father, and knew that she couldn't say anything to jeopardise their plans—much as she would have liked to.

Kirstie still didn't think that spending time with him in Spain was for the best. It would be heaven for her daughter but hell for her, and would Becky notice the antagonism between them? Would it make the holiday uncomfortable?

She glared after him as he slid into his Bentley and started the engine, hating him and yet acknowledging that he could still stir her senses at the same time. When he lifted his hand she didn't wave back. She slammed the door shut instead.

Sitting in the private jet that was whisking them swiftly to their holiday destination, Kirstie felt her animosity towards Lucio hadn't lessened one iota. She'd spent sleepless nights worrying about their impending visit and it was costing her dear.

This jet was the last straw, another indication of Lucio's extravagance. He lived a lifestyle far removed from her own and it was not what she wanted for her daughter. Becky, on the other hand, was lapping it up. First a Range Rover had arrived to pick them up, and now this plane. Becky was so excited she couldn't sit still, but as far as Kirstie was concerned all Lucio was trying to do was impress.

Kirstie wanted to warn her but knew that Becky wouldn't listen to a bad word said about him, not at this early stage. As far as Becky was concerned, Lucio couldn't put a foot wrong.

They'd sat talking about him after that first meeting and Becky hadn't been able to understand why her mother had finished with him. She thought he was the most gorgeous father ever and Kirstie knew that she needed to find out for herself that relationships came secondary in his life. Nevertheless she was determined to do all she could to protect her daughter.

Or was it herself who needed protection? Lucio was a darkly dangerous man, well-aware of his own sexuality and the effect it had on the opposite sex. She hadn't believed for one second his excuse that his kiss was innocent. He had been trying it on. Even in his teenage years girls had flocked around him like butterflies—and they still did. He probably thought he could have any woman he wanted.

Well, not this one!

Not any more!

As the plane began to lose height Kirstie felt her heart sinking in unison. She was not looking forward to this holiday, not one little bit, and if it hadn't been for Becky she would have asked the pilot to turn around and take them home again. Unfortunately that was not one of her options.

She expected to be met by a car and driver, and horrified herself by accepting that this was a way of life for them now. But after they'd cleared Customs she was astonished to see Lucio himself waiting for them.

In fitted black trousers and a black polo shirt, he looked stunningly handsome. His thick dark hair was ruffled, as though he'd impatiently brushed his fingers through it as he waited for them, and she could imagine why. Time was money as far as he was concerned. She should be flattered that he'd made the effort.

Becky had spotted him too and was off at a run, leaving her mother to follow more slowly. It annoyed Kirstie when her heartbeats quickened. Sixteen years should have been more than enough to get this man out of her system.

'Welcome,' he said in his deep, sexy voice when she joined them. 'My car is waiting; let's go.' He took control of the luggage and in no time at all they were on their way.

The air outside was hot and humid but in his car, a sleek white monster this time, it was blessedly cool. 'How was your flight?' Even though dark glasses hid his eyes, when Lucio looked at her through the rear-view mirror Kirstie felt ice slither down her spine and her heart sink shakily into her stomach. This man was far too dangerous for her peace of mind. How could she hate him and yet feel pulled towards him at the same time? It didn't make sense.

And the fact that she was here in his car, speeding towards his Spanish home, didn't make sense either. For her daughter's sake she would remain civil to him, but it would be difficult, if not impossible.

'Very comfortable, thank you,' she answered carefully. She didn't want to sound too enthusiastic. She had never been in a private plane before and had been totally awestruck. Instead of rows of seats it had actual rooms, with soft-footed stewards attending to her every whim! She couldn't ask for the wrong thing. It had a bathroom to die for and even a library. And an office, of course, almost a boardroom with its oblong table and chairs, which she presumed Lucio used whenever he was travelling. He wouldn't want to waste all those precious hours.

'You had everything you wanted?'

If she said no, would heads roll? 'Thank you, yes.'

Becky was sitting at her side this time, but she seemed not to be listening, intent instead on the rolling scenery. They had been to Spain on holiday before but never to this mountainous region and even Kirstie began to feel excited. 'Where are we going?'

'To my mountain retreat,' he informed her, his eyes meeting hers challengingly through the mirror. At least challenge was what she felt. And the word retreat didn't exactly fill her with enthusiasm.

'What do you mean?'

'I have two homes here. One in Barcelona, near the European hub of my business, and one here for when I feel a need to get away from it all.'

Get away from it all! Kirstie couldn't believe that she was hearing him correctly. This man was a workaholic. Why would he need to escape? And the thought of going to some isolated place filled her with fear. 'Is that very fair on Becky?' she asked, her tone intentionally sharp.

'Do not fear. There's a village near by where she'll not be short of company. But in any case, the whole idea of this holiday is for me to get to know my daughter.'

'What do you think, Becky?' she asked, demanding her daughter's attention. 'Do you fancy some isolated place in the mountains? Or the fast life of a big city?'

'Do you have a swimming pool at your mountain retreat?' asked Becky longingly. Swimming was her favourite hobby.

'I do,' he confirmed.

'And horses?'

'Yes.'

'Then I vote for the mountain.'

Kirstie knew she had lost.

* * *

Lucio was looking forward to getting to know his new daughter and was glad that she approved of his plans. He'd been apprehensive over their first meeting, wondering whether Rebecca would even like him, or whether he'd take to her. Having a fifteen-year-old daughter foisted on him was not something he had ever considered. But he had worried for nothing; she was a lovely, well-adjusted girl who had unreservedly accepted him, and his world had changed overnight.

When he'd told his parents the news it had been greeted by blank dismay from his mother but his father had chuckled delightedly. They had met Kirstie briefly during the few short months he'd gone out with her, and his mother hadn't exactly taken to her. Now his parents lived here in Spain, which was his mother's birth country, and he was looking forward to introducing their granddaughter to them.

But first of all he wanted time with Rebecca himself. There were so many things he wanted to find out about his daughter, and she too must be dying of curiosity. She was fifteen, coming sixteen. Kirstie had been seventeen when they met. Hardly any difference in their ages, but a whole world of difference in their attitude towards life!

Kirstie had been incredibly shy, but so beautiful that he hadn't been able to take his eyes off her. She had the most amazing amethyst eyes, wide and luminous and thickly lashed. And rich auburn hair that flowed over her shoulders like a river of copper.

He had known from the first time he saw her that he had wanted her. And she had blossomed like a flower in the spring when they had started going out together, her shyness vanishing as she got to know him better. He had been her first lover and when they finally went to bed together she had shown a voracious sexual appetite and could never get enough of him. Or he of her if the truth were known!

In all the years since he had never met anyone quite like her.

Glancing at Kirstie now through the mirror made him wonder why he had ever been foolish enough to let her go. Surely he could have managed to combine work and play? Or would he have been so focused on his future that he would have failed to nurture their relationship? Would he have lost her anyway? And would it have hurt even more if they'd had a few years together?

He was angry with her for keeping Rebecca a secret, deeply angry; but despite that he still found her stunningly attractive. When she walked towards him at the airport, tall and proud in a floaty pink summer dress and high-heeled sandals, he had been wowed anew by her beauty.

When he hit a pothole and jolted his passengers Lucio knew that he'd better keep his eyes on the road. He could hear mother and daughter talking quietly as Rebecca pointed out things of interest, and an hour later they had reached their destination.

His house nestled on a pine-clad hillside and Rebecca jumped excitedly out of the car almost before it stopped.

'This is it,' said Lucio, turning to look at Kirstie, who had made no attempt to move.

'It's very isolated.'

'The village is only a mile away.' They had actually passed through it on their way.

'Do you spend much time here?'

'A few weeks every year.'

'I'm amazed.'

'I thought you might be.' She was so hostile towards him, and had it firmly fixed in her mind that he was a workaholic who never took a minute's time off, that he wondered whether he was making a grave mistake, whether the atmosphere would be unhealthy for his daughter. Perhaps he should have taken them straight to Barcelona, where at least his mother and father could have helped to ease any disharmony between them.

Silently Kirstie followed Lucio towards the house. It stood three storeys high and she guessed that the upper rooms would have commanding views over the surrounding countryside. Under different circumstances, if there were no hostilities between them, she would have been excited. She could hear trickling water and caught a glint of it through the trees. It was an idyllic spot really—for people in love!

But you'd have to love a person very much to live in such a remote hideaway. Did Lucio really spend time here alone, or was it a secret love nest? She would probably never know, and did she really want to?

Inside the rooms were spacious and minimally furnished. Kirstie liked it much better than his London home. On the ground floor was an open-plan living area and a kitchen to die for. On the first floor were two *en suite* bedrooms.

'For you and Rebecca,' Lucio said as he gave them the grand tour.

The whole of the top floor was taken up by the master bedroom with windows on all sides and a wide balcony from which the views, as Kirstie had imagined, were truly magnificent.

'What do you think?' he asked.

'It's fabulous!' declared Rebecca. 'And look, Mum, there's the swimming pool. Isn't it fantastic?'

It was a D-shaped pool jutting out from the house at the back, set into a terrace where chairs and loungers were invitingly placed.

'Go and take a look,' encouraged Lucio. 'Explore as much as you like.'

Rebecca galloped down the stairs and Kirstie started to follow. It was only just beginning to hit her how much time she would have to spend alone with Lucio. She didn't want that. It would be fatal. 'I think I'll go and unpack,' she said faintly.

Lucio put a hand on her shoulder, a gentle touch and yet it felt like a vice. 'I don't want there to be any awkwardness between us.' And he turned her to face him. 'Rebecca's a sensitive girl; she'll soon pick up on it. I want her to enjoy her time here.'

'Which she will,' announced Kirstie crisply, shrugging him off and taking a step back. How the hell did he know Becky was sensitive? He'd spent so little time with her that he couldn't possibly know.

But actually there was no fear of her daughter doing anything other than enjoy herself. A pool to swim in whenever she liked! A horse at her disposal somewhere, though she hadn't seen any sign of one yet. The only person who was going to be unhappy was herself. There'd been no mention of a mountain hideaway when he first mentioned a holiday. 'Did you plan all along to bring us here?'

'I did.' Dark eyes narrowed. 'Do you have a problem with it?'

Of course she did. It was too intimate. There was nowhere for her to go to get away from him. 'It's not what I expected. I think you should have told us.'

'Rebecca likes it.'

'So you're doing what I feared most, buying her love? Tempting her with a pool and a horse to ride and lord knows what else you have up your sleeve.' Purple eyes flashed accusingly and she felt like beating her hands against his chest, but knew that if she did he would catch hold of them and pull her close—and probably kiss her again!

A spiral of sensations whirled and twirled through every limb. She hated to admit even to herself that this was what she feared most of all. She would be putty in his hands if he dared so much as to touch his lips to her skin. Even a feather-light touch would be her undoing. It would take every ounce of strength and courage to resist him. She dashed the feelings away by stalking across the room to look out of one of the other windows.

From here the pine forest climbed high above them, almost obliterating the intense blue of the sky.

'This is my lifestyle, Kirstie. I was hoping that you'd be proud that I've achieved so much.'

'I am impressed,' she admitted, 'but I can't help but wonder at what expense.' She swung around to face him. 'You're not married, you have three homes that I know of, maybe more, and yet you live alone. What sort of a life is that?'

There was a long silence before he answered and Kirstie wondered if she had hit a raw nerve.

'And who are you to criticise my lifestyle?' he demanded, pure ice in his eyes. 'Is there a man in *your* life? No, I thought not. Seems we're two of a kind, Kirstie. So if I were you, I'd think twice before you condemn me.'

Kirstie stiffened. 'I was *not* condemning. I was merely pointing out a fact.'

'Really?' His arms were once more folded over his hard-muscled chest, feet apart, eyes resolutely on hers. 'It sounded like sour grapes to me. Perhaps you're regretting walking out on me. Perhaps you're thinking that if you'd hung around long enough all of this would have been yours.'

Kirstie shook her head so wildly that her hair swung over her face. She eyed him through the dark curtain. This conversation was getting them nowhere. She really ought to be unpacking their cases and checking to make sure that Becky was OK.

But somehow Lucio had moved between her and the doorway and she instinctively knew that he would not let her go. Exactly what he wanted from her she wasn't sure, but her heart began a drum roll in her chest, and when his hand reached out to lift her hair away from her face Kirstie flinched.

CHAPTER FIVE

KIRSTIE found Becky sitting on the edge of the pool, her feet swinging idly in the water. Kicking off her sandals, she joined her. 'What do you think of it here, darling?'

'It's cool, Mum. Dad must be really rich, mustn't he?'

'Is that why you like him, for his money?' asked Kirstie sharply, unable to help herself. And hating the way her daughter so easily called Lucio Dad.

'I wouldn't care if he was penniless,' answered Becky easily. 'He's my father. I've prayed so hard all these years to meet him. I'm not going to waste a second of the time we spend together.'

Kirstie's stomach gave a sickening lurch. Her daughter had just put her well and truly in her place for leaving it until now to find Lucio. She was getting it on both sides and was almost beginning to wish that she hadn't given in to her conscience and contacted him.

She certainly wouldn't be in the predicament she was in now.

When Lucio had slowly and deliberately moved her hair back from her face her whole body had tingled in anticipation of what was to come next. His eyes, cold as flint, had locked into hers, locked and held, so that she was powerless to look away. And unhurriedly he had cupped her chin, his hand cool and yet burning her flesh at the same time, tilting her head so that he could look all the better into her face.

'I know you don't want to be here, Kirstie. But since you are, my advice to you would be to make the most of it.'

'And that includes precisely what?' she riposted. 'Giving myself to you?' The words were out before Kirstie could stop them and her cheeks burned for a very different reason this time.

'If that's what you want I can easily oblige,' he answered evenly, with not a hint of a smile on his lips. They merely wavered at the corners but his eyes were still dark and expressionless. 'It's not what I meant, though. I want you to enjoy yourself. This is a holiday for you as well as Rebecca. I thought you would like it here. It's smaller, and cosier, and…'

He let his voice trail away, he even dropped his hand from her chin, but Kirstie couldn't move. His gaze trapped her like a doe caught in a car's headlights, the heat of his body drawing her inexorably closer. Her breasts swelled and hardened, her nipples grew taut and excitement stirred in her most private of places.

Something invisible and intangible bound her to him. She couldn't move a limb, not even utter a word. When she heard Lucio's soft sigh, when the scent of him invaded her nostrils as he drew that little bit closer, Kirstie knew that she was lost.

She closed her eyes, as if by so doing she could shut out what was going to happen next. Because whatever did happen would not be of her own making! It was as though some supreme power had taken hold of her body and was telling her that it was all right to let go; that this man wasn't her enemy, he was her ex-lover, a fantastic lover, and that he could be so again.

Hadn't she enjoyed his body? Hadn't she found in herself a voracious appetite for sex? Didn't she want it again? Didn't she want to feel the pulsing hardness of him inside her, urging her to heights she had never dreamed possible?

The answer was yes, yes, yes! But only in her dreams! Not in real life. Not here and now with their daughter likely to put in an appearance at any second.

But when she felt herself pulled against the hard wall of his chest, when she felt the hammer beat of his heart, when she felt the hardness of him against her stomach, every resolution winged its way out of the window. Every fear and every doubt was forgotten.

He held her close and they swayed to the musical sound of the wind in the pines and the crystal tinkle of a distant waterfall. The only barrier between them was their clothes. Had circumstances been different Kirstie knew that they would have been ripped off by now. She recalled Lucio cradling her like this once before when pan pipes were playing on the radio. The music had been hauntingly erotic and they had ended up going to bed.

It was this thought that made her snap out of her hypnotic trance and push her hands hard against his chest. 'What the hell do you think you're doing?'

He let her go immediately but a slow smile lifted the corners of his mouth, even though his eyes were still hard and disturbing on hers. 'It takes two to tango,' he taunted.

'So this is the reason you brought us here?' She stood tall and proud and indignant, her eyes shimmering purple anger. 'I knew I was making a mistake. In fact I made a mistake in telling you that you had a daughter. If it wasn't for the fact that Becky's so excited, so thrilled that she's finally met you, I'd leave this very second.'

'It's a long walk.'

'And that's what you're relying on, isn't it?' Kirstie's whole body grew rigid with resentment. 'We're trapped here.'

'You're even more beautiful than you were at seventeen.'

His sudden change of subject took Kirstie by surprise. 'Flattery will get you nowhere.'

'And I hope you were joking when you said that you wished you hadn't told me about Rebecca.' His jaw tensed and his voice rasped so sharply that it hurt Kirstie's nerve ends. 'It's bad enough that you left it for fifteen years. If I'd ever found out before then your life would have been hell. What kind of mother are you? You deny your daughter her father, and you deny a father his daughter. What were you thinking?'

He hadn't waited for her answer, he'd merely whirled on his heel and left, and it was several minutes later before Kirstie found the strength to go to her room and unpack, and finally join her daughter at the poolside.

'What are you thinking about, Mum?'

'What a lovely place it is here,' she lied.

'You look sad.'

'Just memories.'

'Of my father?'

Kirstie nodded.

'I wish you two hadn't broken up. He's everything I've ever wanted in a father.'

You don't know him yet, thought Kirstie sadly. He had looks and wealth, but feelings? There'd not been much proof of those. His only emotions were physical ones. He had a high sex drive, proved by how many times he'd been pictured in the media with a pretty girl on his arm. And their relationship, too, had been all about sex.

She'd been too young to realise it at the time. She'd thought he loved her, and she had been sure that she was in love with him. But in actual fact all that they'd had between them was a chemical attraction. Unfortunately it was still there and, given half a chance, Lucio wouldn't be afraid to take advantage.

'Take time to get to know him,' warned Kirstie gently.

Becky frowned. 'Because you two split up doesn't mean to say he and I won't get on. I hope you're not going to spoil things for me, Mum.'

'Of course not,' said Kirstie at once. 'I want you to love your father and I want Lucio to love you. All I'm saying is that it's early days. Take things one step at a time. He's a very busy man; he won't always have time to spend with you.'

'I'm not stupid, Mum. I know he's putting himself out to make time to get to know me, and I appreciate that. I also know that there'll be times when I won't see him for weeks because he'll be off on one of his business trips. So you've nothing to worry about.'

'Well said.'

Again Lucio had silently crept up on them and Kirstie couldn't help wondering how much of the conversation he'd heard.

The next second there was a splash as he dived into the pool. They both watched as he swam an impressive length underwater. When he resurfaced he shook the water from his hair before asking, 'Isn't anyone going to join me?'

'I will,' said Becky at once. 'Give me two seconds to get changed.' And she was away to her room with lightning speed.

'Aren't you coming in too?' His voice deepened into a sensual growl.

'Not today,' Kirstie answered. Not with Lucio, not when the chemistry she'd been thinking about earlier rose in her body until it totally consumed her. Tension tightened every limb as her eyes unwillingly drifted over him. His body had matured magnificently; broader and harder-muscled than before, with a deep tan that spoke of many hours spent out of doors. Perhaps here! But with whom? Kirstie was consumed with curiosity. She found it hard to believe that he would spend time here alone. His retreat, he'd said, but it didn't make sense.

She watched, mesmerised, as crystal-clear drops of water dripped from his hair to his shoulders and then slide in sparkling rivulets down the smooth hardness of his chest. How tempted she was to lean forward and touch, to stroke her fingers over his skin and feel once again his vital maleness.

Unaware that her breathing had deepened, she saw only that Lucio's eyes had narrowed knowingly on her face. He inched closer towards her, so casually that she didn't even register it until his hands gripped the edge of the pool on either side of her, effectively making her his prisoner.

The air around her thickened and Kirstie would have given anything to make her escape. She felt like a caged bird, her heart fluttering violently in her breast, her agitated fingers automatically going out to touch Lucio's shoulders and push him away.

A futile exercise! Lucio's strength was far superior. Eyes as dark as pitch locked into hers, sending unspoken signals of need and desire; telling her that, although he could do nothing about it now, the time was not far off when he intended renewing his acquaintance with her body.

A shiver ran down Kirstie's spine.

He was instantly attentive. 'Are you cold?'

Canvas sails were stretched across the terrace and part of the pool as protection from the intense heat of the midday sun. But it was a pleasant coolness, and had nothing to do with the ice that was fast gripping her senses. 'Not at all,' she answered; 'just someone walking over my grave.'

'Why don't I believe you?' he asked softly. 'It's still very much alive, isn't it, the powerful attraction we once felt?'

Kirstie had changed into a T-shirt and shorts and now became embarrassingly aware that her nipples had peaked under Lucio's hot gaze and were very much in evidence beneath the soft cotton. 'Maybe it is, maybe it isn't,' she admitted grudgingly, 'but whatever I feel, I have no intention of becoming involved with you again, not in that way. We'll be friends for Becky's sake, but that's all.'

'Maybe you won't be able to help yourself.' Strong fingers caught her wrists, and his thumbs stroked the soft inside skin in an unhurried rhythm.

'And maybe you'll get fed up of trying,' she riposted, trying to force a glassy hardness into her eyes but knowing that she failed miserably. There was no hiding the fact that Lucio's aggressive maleness made nonsense of her protests.

Her pulses beat in a painful rapid rhythm of awareness and her mouth had gone so dry that her tongue edged out to moisten her lips. She wished herself a million miles away and when Lucio drew in a swift breath, his darkened eyes on her temptingly moistened mouth, his head moving purposefully closer, Kirstie knew that he was going to kiss her.

'No!' she cried, and with a strength born of desperation she wrenched her hands free and pushed once more against the hard wall of his chest. It was a futile exercise. His strong arms locked around her and she closed her eyes when his mouth claimed hers. The battle was lost. Red-hot feelings streaked through her, feelings she had thought never to experience again, and she felt herself drowning in a sea of unleashed emotions. Drowning, drowning…

Until she realised that Lucio had slid her into the pool and was kissing her underwater, his hungry hands touching and exploring, while his mouth remained locked on hers. It was an exquisite form of torture and she wondered whether this was what it was like to be a mermaid and live and make love in the ocean.

It seemed like for ever that he kissed and stroked, missing not one part of her body. He brought her to the brink of madness before they both felt their lungs bursting and were compelled to surface for air.

She dragged in deep, hungry breaths, her body pulsing feverishly, and out of the corner of her eye she saw their daughter approaching. 'This is insanity,' she hissed. 'What am I going to tell Becky?'

'Let me handle her,' he answered calmly. 'She'll think that we're kissing and making up.'

'I don't want her to think that,' spat Kirstie, her troubled eyes deeply violet.

His brows drew into a ferocious frown. 'Why not? Wouldn't it be in her best interests?'

'And you really want that, do you?' she snapped, backing away from him and reaching for the edge of the pool. 'You want us to be real parents, to get married and give Becky a stable family life?'

'I wasn't talking about marriage,' he answered grimly.

Kirstie's eyes flashed again. 'No, I didn't think so. Marriage is not on your list of priorities. You enjoy the chase of the game but that's all. You're a swine of the highest order, Lucio Masterton.'

His face darkened ominously. 'Don't push your luck, Kirstie.'

Push her luck? She was in the depths of hell because of him, here under sufferance, and the fact that he'd had the temerity to kiss her sent her blood pressure soaring sky-high. She wanted to spit and scratch like a cat under threat.

'What's happened, Mum?' Becky's eyes were troubled as she surveyed them. 'Why are you in the water with your clothes on?'

Lucio answered for her. 'Because I pulled your mother in,' he said with a laugh, no sign at all that they'd been arguing—or even kissing a few short minutes ago. While Kirstie was all steamed up he'd coolly shrugged everything off.

'Why?'

'Because I said I didn't want to swim,' cut in Kirstie, afraid of what he might say next. 'Your father's powers of persuasion are rather extreme.' And she managed to laugh too, though it hurt her to do so. 'But I think I've had enough already.' She hauled herself out and smiled into her daughter's face. 'You can have him all to yourself.'

'You weren't arguing, Mum?' asked Becky softly.

'Not at all!'

But Becky didn't look convinced and Kirstie sighed as she made her way up to her room, leaving a trail of water on the tiles behind her, muttering under her breath that she hoped Lucio would slip on them and break his neck. Not that she really meant it, but he'd got her so riled up that she could think of nothing but evil thoughts as far as he was concerned.

Even after she'd showered and changed Kirstie felt no better and knew that she needed to get away from the house, if only for a short time. She'd walk into the village, that was what she'd do; leave Becky to get to know her father better.

Without even telling them that she was going out Kirstie strode off down the dusty mountain road. Ten minutes later she reached the village. Plastic bags and beer cans blew against wheelie bins outside a tiny supermarket and even from a few yards away she could breathe in the smell of garlic and coffee. There was a bar next door where old men were gathered, smoking their pipes over a game of cards at a table outside. They looked at her curiously for a moment or two then carried on with their game.

A scrawny dog ambled across the road and sniffed around her ankles before wandering back to his shady spot against the wall. Another shop sold second-hand furniture, and she found a butcher's and a baker's and amazingly a shoe shop, though she couldn't think that they'd do much trade. Unless she was underestimating the size of the population in this area!

On either side of the road cubes of houses sprawled up the mountainside. None so fine as Lucio's, and she wondered what they thought of this half-Spaniard half-Englishman who had chosen to live here for part of each year.

She walked into the *farmacia* and was treated to the same enquiring stare as she'd had from the old men. *'Quiero algo para las picaduras de insecto, por favor,'* she said haltingly, hoping she'd got it right. During their last visit to Spain she and Becky had both learned some phrase-book Spanish, and, as she'd already been bitten on her walk to the village, Kirstie thought she ought to get some insect spray in readiness for further attacks.

'You Engleesh?' asked the middle-aged lady behind the counter.

'Si.'

'I speak Engleesh.' She sounded proud of the fact. 'You 'ere on 'oliday?'

Kirstie nodded. 'With Lucio Masterton from the big house up the mountain.'

'Ah, *si.*' A broad grin came over her face. 'He is nice man. He spend money 'ere in village. You 'is wife?'

'No!' Kirstie shook her head firmly.

'A friend! I see.' The woman's eyes twinkled and it was

clear that she thought Kirstie was Lucio's current girlfriend, and that she thought the world of Lucio too.

'Do you have any insect repellent?' repeated Kirstie, not wanting to talk about Lucio.

'Si,' said the woman reaching for an aerosol spray.

It was not until then that Kirstie realised she had forgotten to bring her euros. 'I'm sorry,' she said, 'I cannot pay. I have only English money.'

'No problem,' said the woman at once. 'You pay next time.'

Clearly Lucio's name was enough, thought Kirstie as she left the shop after thanking the woman profusely. If she hadn't been so annoyed with him she would have been impressed. As it was she'd felt like declining the spray can, except that it might have led to awkward questions.

Slowly she made her way back towards the villa, in time to see Lucio driving like a maniac towards her. He skidded to a halt at her side. 'What the hell are you doing?'

'I've been shopping,' she told him lightly. 'Except stupidly I forgot my euros! The woman in the chemist's said that I could settle up next time.'

Lucio frowned harshly. 'Jump in.'

'I prefer to walk.'

'I said, jump in.' Anger darkened his face and, although Kirstie wanted to refuse, she thought better of it.

He raced down to the village, took some small change into the *farmacia* and then bounced back into the car. 'Next time you think of going somewhere, tell me first,' he snarled, reversing fiercely before putting his foot hard down on the throttle to roar his way back up the mountain.

'I can't see a problem with what I did. I didn't go far.'

'Far enough for me to worry about you!'

'Why? What harm could I come to?'

'Dammit, Kirstie, are you out of your mind? Anything could have happened. You could have gone wandering over the mountain and slipped and broken a leg or something. It could have been hours before I found you.'

'But I didn't, did I?' she yelled back. 'I was perfectly safe.' And he was behaving as though he cared! Or was it because he felt responsible for her? Nothing more, nothing less! He had brought her here; it was his job to make sure she came to no harm.

Damn the man! 'Where's Becky?' she asked, knowing it was a stupid question, that Becky would be perfectly safe. But it would help if she could make him feel as guilty as he was trying to make her.

'Becky's all right. Worried about you, but OK.'

They reached the villa and her daughter came running out. 'Mum, where've you been? We were so worried.'

'I just took a stroll into the village, darling. There was no need to panic. I needed some insect repellent.'

'Which I already have in my medicine cabinet,' Lucio informed her curtly. 'Next time you decide to go walkies, tell me first,' he repeated. And with that parting shot he stormed indoors.

CHAPTER SIX

FURY filled every one of Lucio's veins as he took the stairs two at a time up to his room. It coursed through him like lava flowing from a volcano, hot and liquid and very, very dangerous.

Kirstie was here under sufferance; he realised that. Here because she didn't want to let her daughter out of her sight. He still found it hard to believe that she had kept him in ignorance of his progeny all these years. The thought of it was like a knife slicing through his heart. It hurt so much that he thought it would kill him.

And Kirstie had just made it absolutely clear that she didn't want to be in the same house as him, let alone in close proximity. How damning was that? But was it really necessary for her to show her dislike in front of Rebecca? Didn't she realise the danger? Didn't she know what it was doing to their daughter?

Rebecca had been close to tears when they had discovered that Kirstie was missing and she confessed that she had heard them arguing when she came out to the pool. He had done his best to persuade her that he and her mother weren't deadly enemies, but she hadn't been convinced.

And in all truthfulness he couldn't blame her. The hostility between them was thick enough to be visible by the naked eye—and not only on Kirstie's side. As far as he was concerned she had done the unforgivable and he would never get over it. He would resent her for ever more.

Though why she was equally hostile towards him he didn't know. Had she carried this antagonism all these years, ever since she'd discovered that she was pregnant? What he couldn't understand was why she had never told him. Did she really think that he would have turned his back on her? It proved how little she knew him.

He had adored Kirstie, but he just hadn't felt ready to commit to a serious relationship. Not at nineteen, when he'd got his whole career to think about. In his mind it had been important to be successful, to be able to provide for a wife and children, not live in some dreary bedsit because it was the best they could afford.

Somewhere in the back of his mind had lived a faint hope that one day they would get back together. But never had he dreamt that it would be in this way.

He showered and dressed ready for their evening meal but even when he went back downstairs his thoughts were black and bitter.

Kirstie didn't come out of her room until Becky tapped on the door and told her that dinner was ready. She felt like refusing; food was the last thing on her mind. The full focus of her attention was on the fact that she had made a big mistake coming here. It would have been far better to let Becky come alone. Except that she'd have worried even more!

The fact that she still felt this ridiculously strong attraction to Lucio was playing havoc with her nerves, and she feared for her sanity in the ensuing days. There was no escape from him, nowhere to go, nothing to do except swim together, horse ride together, walk together. If only Becky had opted for his house in Barcelona; at least then she could have explored the sights of the city—there would have been lots of things to do that were denied her here.

'I wish that you still loved my father,' said Becky as they made their way downstairs.

Kirstie looked at her daughter sharply. 'What's he been saying to you?'

'Nothing.' Becky shrugged her narrow shoulders. 'But it's perfectly clear that you're not happy here. I thought that…' Her voice trailed away sadly.

'You thought what?'

'That when you two met up again everything would be OK. You must have loved him once, and I have a sneaky feeling that he still loves you.'

'Nonsense!' snapped Kirstie. 'Your father has never loved me. And you might as well know now that he never will. Work is your father's love; making money. Not that it's brought him much happiness, but—'

'But you had *me*,' declared Becky, her voice breaking on a sob. 'He must have felt something for you, and you for him.'

'People don't always have babies because they're in love, Becky. You're old enough to know that. I made a big mistake with your father. I thought myself in love, that's true, but I wasn't. I was too young to know the real meaning of the word. And I hope, my darling, that you never make the same mistake.'

'I won't, Mum,' said Becky. 'I promise. And if you don't love my father, would it be too much to ask for you to be friends?'

Kirstie felt as though she'd been slapped on the wrist and told that she'd been a naughty girl. Poor Becky! Her daughter was suffering because of her own selfish behaviour and she'd been too blind to see it. She pasted a big smile on her lips. 'We're not enemies, I assure you of that.' No woman in her right mind would want to go to bed with her enemy.

Becky would never know what she really thought of Lucio, realised Kirstie. Feelings far too intimate to be discussed filled every inch of her body whenever he was near, and when he wasn't present he still crept into her thoughts. It made a mess of her whole system and pretending for her daughter's sake that nothing was wrong was going to be the hardest thing she'd ever had to do.

For some reason Kirstie had assumed that Lucio would cook their evening meal—she could remember him rustling up all sorts of food in his student days, some of it appetising, some not—and she was surprised to see another woman in the kitchen.

'Kirstie, this is Dolores,' introduced Lucio. 'She comes and looks after me whenever I'm here.'

The woman smiled and looked at her curiously, and Kirstie couldn't help wondering how many other women he had brought here. Dolores looked to be in her late forties, slim, good-looking once, though her beauty was fading, but with a smile that lit up her whole face.

'Dolores doesn't speak English,' Lucio told her, and then turned to the woman and said something in Spanish. Kirstie was impressed, although, if he had two houses here, and a business base, it made sense that he would need to be able to speak the language.

'I thought we'd eat outside,' he said. Dark eyes regarded her coolly, as though he expected her to object.

Kirstie smiled pleasantly, remembering her daughter's request. 'That would be lovely. We have so little opportunity in England for dining alfresco. Is there anything I can do?'

A dark brow rose. Why, it asked, was she suddenly being nice? 'Not at all!' he replied evenly. 'I hope you're hungry; Dolores has cooked enough to feed an army.'

'I'm starving,' said Becky.

Kirstie remained noncommittal. In fact, she doubted whether she could manage even one bite.

The table had been laid on the terrace by the pool, with a perfect view of the distant mountains. It was a heavenly place and Kirstie could see why Lucio had chosen it as his retreat. He took his seat at the head of the oblong table, leaving Kirstie and Becky to sit on either side of him.

As far as Kirstie was concerned, he was too close for comfort. She could feel a fiery heat emanating from him—or was it the other way round? Whatever, she felt distinctly uncomfortable, especially when he reached out and took her hand and then Becky's. 'You've made my life complete,' he said gruffly.

Kirstie was instantly on her guard but when she looked into her daughter's face Becky was beaming happily. As if knowing that Kirstie would not be so receptive, Lucio squeezed her hand warningly, and although her face felt stiff and unresponsive she managed to stretch her mouth into a smile, but she snatched her hand free as soon as she could safely do so.

'Are you allowed wine?' he asked Becky, lifting a bottle from the ice bucket at his side.

Becky glanced at her mother, seemed about to say yes, she would try some; then shook her head. 'Not yet! Not till I'm eighteen. I'll have water, please.'

'Did you have this villa built to your own specifications?' asked Kirstie after he had poured their drinks, anxious to ease the tension that was hovering over them like a ball of fire.

'I did. Do you approve?' There was nothing in his expression to suggest that he was still angry with her. Indeed his smile was pleasant and friendly and as long as she played her part Becky would never guess at the animosity simmering beneath the surface.

'It's lovely,' she said, firing her voice with enthusiasm, 'although I would never have imagined that you'd be happy somewhere like this. In my mind you're the high-flying businessman who spends his life flitting from meeting to meeting and never has time to relax.'

'Everyone needs to relax at some time,' he said, his sepia eyes intent on hers, seeing right into her soul, knowing that she was making an extreme effort.

Kirstie felt a *frisson* of awareness and when she glanced across at her daughter she saw that Becky was watching them. If she wanted to keep her daughter happy she needed to act as she had never acted before in her life.

'Of course,' she said softly. 'And what better place? I love it here already.'

'Do you holiday often?'

'Once a year, in Becky's main school holidays.'

'And where do you go?'

'We used to go on caravan holidays in England but lately we've been travelling to Europe.' Since her business had taken off and money wasn't so tight! 'Mainly Spain; the Blancas or Benidorm—somewhere lively for Becky.'

'Do you like Spain?' Lucio turned his attention to his daughter.

'I love it,' answered Becky with a big grin. 'I love anywhere abroad.'

'You don't like England?'

'Of course I do, Dad; you know what I mean.'

He laughed. 'You'll have the best of both worlds now.'

Kirstie felt an ominous shiver slide down her spine and curl around her stomach. He was tempting her again with his money and his power. 'Don't forget Becky's education comes before holidays.'

'Naturally, I would never take her away from that, Kirstie; you have my word.' His smile was dazzlingly white and friendly. It even reached his eyes.

Kirstie could not help smiling in response, her fear changing to something warmer and intoxicating, a well-remembered feeling that could easily take over her whole body. He was doing it deliberately, she knew that, but even so it was working. His magic was weaving its way through her limbs, curling her toes and scrunching her stomach, sending little trembles of anticipation right from the base of her throat down to the heart of her desire.

And there was not a thing she could do about it! Not in front of their daughter. Her natural instinct was to get up and run but already Dolores was approaching. *'Que aproveche,'* she said, after she had laid out an assortment of dishes. Enjoy your meal!

The food was delicious, especially the chicken paella, and considering she'd had no appetite Kirstie did more than justice to it. She also drank more wine than was wise, and felt flushed and happy afterwards.

She was surprised when Becky announced that she was going to bed, though she guessed that it was an excuse to leave the two of them alone. As the evening had progressed, and they had drunk more and more wine, she and Lucio had grown warmer and warmer towards each other, and she imagined that their daughter had noticed.

Dolores cleared the table and they moved to another area of the terrace, where comfortable leather chairs were arranged in an intimate group.

'You've thought of everything here, haven't you?' she asked quietly.

'I like my creature comforts.'

You and who else? she couldn't help wondering. This was most certainly not a bachelor pad. But she pushed her thoughts behind her. What did it matter whom he entertained?

Not a jot, said the sane part of her mind, but her more emotional side, heightened by the amount of alcohol she'd consumed, couldn't help feeling a stab of jealousy. It was ridiculous when they'd spent sixteen years apart. What had she expected—that Lucio would live like a monk?

'Would you like anything else to drink? I can open more wine, or—'

'No, thanks,' cut in Kirstie emphatically. 'I've already had more than I'm used to.'

'If it's helped you relax then it has to be a good thing. You're looking more at home every minute.'

The aggressive masculinity of his face, the whiteness of his smile, caused butterflies to flutter in her stomach. Actually they did more than flutter; they stampeded. 'It's for Becky's sake,' she informed him tightly, deliberately stamping on her feelings, not wanting him to guess the way she felt, or to even think that he was gaining in popularity.

'Nevertheless it has to be good.' He moved his chair a few inches closer and in the night air the musky smell of his cologne intensified, drifting over her, wrapping itself around her, bonding her to him. It was madness. She couldn't move, it was difficult to even breathe, and she desperately wished that she had joined her daughter. They'd had a long day; it would have been a good enough excuse. Instead she had allowed herself to be manipulated into this dangerous situation.

Above them the first stars were turning the sky into a curtain of diamonds; the smell of pine mingled with Lucio's cologne. It was a perfect evening for lovers!

Kirstie shivered.

'Are you cold?' There was genuine concern in his rich voice, which had gone down several octaves since they'd been alone.

'I'm tired,' she said, hoping he would take the hint and suggest that she go up to her room. This situation was getting far too intimate. She liked it better when they were at loggerheads. At least then her insides didn't turn to mush and scare her half to death in the process. Well, not so much anyway.

Lucio nodded his head in agreement. 'Understandably so. But you can relax now. Rebecca's in bed, the night is young and we have a lot of talking to do.'

Kirstie frowned. 'About what?' Their daughter? Her heartbeats surged painfully. Was he planning to take Becky off her? Woo her with riches, make her an impossible-to-refuse offer?

'About you.'

Some of Kirstie's apprehension evaporated. 'Me?'

'I want to know what you've been doing all these years, except bringing up my daughter, of course.'

Bringing up *his* daughter. How it rankled when he said that. But she let it pass; no use starting an argument.

'You have a very nice house,' he went on. 'The money for that had to have come from somewhere. You must have an excellent job. You wanted to be a teacher, isn't that so?'

Kirstie was amazed that he'd remembered and that their conversations hadn't disappeared into the mists of time. 'I did, but I gave up on the idea. I work—' she hesitated for a second, knowing that he would be instantly alert '—in the computer industry.'

She was right; he sat up that little bit straighter and looked at her. 'How interesting; we're both in the same line of business. What do you do exactly?'

Kirstie chose not to look at him, staring up at the stars instead. The sky was a pale violet colour, edging towards purple. She would have liked to comment on it, say how dramatic it was instead of answering him, because she knew exactly where all this was going to lead. 'I write software programmes.'

'Indeed!' She had really caught his attention now. 'Are you good at it?'

'Some people say so.'

'Would you like a job?'

His question took Kirstie by surprise. 'Working for you? No, thank you.' This was an offer she hadn't envisaged.

He frowned. 'You say that as though it would be abhorrent. I pay good money.'

'I'm sure you do,' she answered evenly. 'You get good returns too. Your leap to success has been phenomenal.'

'So you've kept your eye on what I've been doing?' he asked with a predatory gleam in his eyes.

Kirstie cursed beneath her breath. She hadn't meant to give herself away. 'Who can help reading about you?' she asked with a careless shrug. 'Your affairs are always being reported. The Press have a field-day where you're concerned.'

'Unfortunately,' he agreed grimly. 'But we're digressing. It's you we're talking about. What company do you work for?'

'I work for myself.' She said it quietly in the hope that he wouldn't hear, that they could gloss over it and talk about something else. But she had no such luck. Lucio's hearing was as acute as that of a night animal on the prowl.

He rolled his chair round to face her now, eyes alert and interested, his feet touching hers.

'This gets more amazing by the second. You're in business

for yourself? Congratulations, Kirstie. I'm pleased for you. I never realised that you had ambitions too.'

'It wasn't about ambition,' retorted Kirstie, her eyes flashing, 'it was necessity. I was a single mum, don't forget. I didn't want to go out to work and leave Becky with childminders. I worked freelance for a while. But then I thought, why am I doing this, why am I making money for other people? So I set up in business.' And please don't ask any more questions, she prayed.

Lucio's mouth compressed into one of the grim lines she was becoming familiar with. 'Single motherhood wasn't forced on you.'

'I know. It was my choice.'

'Damn you, Kirstie. There shouldn't have been a choice. You should have told me.'

Kirstie sucked in an angry breath. 'It's all water under the bridge. What's the point in railing against it? I did what I thought was right at the time. Let's face it, you wouldn't have been very happy if I'd saddled you with a child while you were still at university. Bang would have gone your studies. Bang would have gone your career. You'd have hated me.'

And when he didn't answer, when his face grew hard and emotionless, Kirstie knew that she was right.

'Tell me more about your business,' he said after a long moment's silence.

'There's nothing more to tell,' she answered.

'What's your firm called? Maybe I've heard of it.'

It was the very question she feared most. 'KR Software.'

Dark eyes narrowed and Kirstie felt the hairs on the back of her neck stand to attention.

'*KR* Software?' he queried, enunciating each letter so that there was no mistaking that he had heard correctly.

She nodded.

'*You* are KR?'

'Yes. K for Kirstie, R for Rebecca,' she informed, her eyes a deep purple as they looked discordantly into his. 'So now you know.'

Several years ago she had written a piece of software to make things easier for people who were just starting out in computers. All they had to do was slip in the disc and it took them every step of the way. She had been thinking of her parents at the time, although unhappily they had died before it was launched.

It was assumed that most people knew what they were doing when they bought a computer, but unless they joined classes or took a home course that wasn't always the case. Her programme had revolutionised the way people learned to use computers. It explained everything in simple language and had been hailed a complete success.

Lucio's company had wanted to buy the rights to her programme. Kirstie had flatly refused. It was a huge amount of money they had been offering, but it wouldn't have been her baby any longer. So she had kept it, and her profits were hugely satisfactory.

'You wrote *Learn to Compute*?'

'Yes.'

Lucio's brows dragged together in a ferocious frown. 'And it was a deliberate act on your part to refuse me the rights?'

She nodded, still with her eyes locked into his. It pleased her that it still rankled even after all these years. She had wanted to hurt him, to hit back at him for hurting her, and it looked as though she had succeeded beyond her wildest dreams.

CHAPTER SEVEN

KIRSTIE lifted her chin and looked at Lucio challengingly. 'Aren't you going to congratulate me?'

'Congratulate you?' he barked. 'I could strangle you.'

Of course he wouldn't congratulate her; he'd failed to win a good business opportunity. She actually felt very smug that she'd got one up on the great Lucio Masterton.

'You're a woman of mystery these days, Kirstie. Is there anything else you haven't told me? Maybe you have a boyfriend skulking somewhere in the background? Someone else bringing up my child?' His voice became dangerously hard and bitingly accusatorial.

'What if there is?' she challenged, both her voice and eyes brittle. 'There's nothing you can do about it.'

Leaning forward so that their knees pressed together, Lucio captured her hands and pulled her forward, his face mere inches from hers. 'I can do anything I want, Kirstie. You'd better remember that.'

Anger pulsed between them like a loudly beating heart and Kirstie wanted to snatch her hands away and run up to her room. Instead she held his gaze and to her horror felt her anger turning to excitement. It trembled through her veins and filled her whole body with electric desire. It was too late to move; she could only hope that Lucio wouldn't notice the effect he was having on her.

'Tell me,' he said, 'who's running your business while you're away?'

'Nice of you to think of that,' she answered with a mocking lift of a fine brow. 'I have a very capable PA who can handle most things. And he has my mobile number in case there are problems.'

'He?' echoed Lucio, letting go of her hands and frowning harshly.

Kirstie enjoyed seeing the shock on his face. 'Jonathon, yes.' She had known Jonathon all her life—they'd lived next to each other when they were kids, gone to the same school, moved in the same circles; he was a very loyal friend and when he was made redundant she had offered him a job. Now she didn't know what she would do without him. 'I also have a male assistant who does my accounting and sees to the legal side of things for me. He would be the one you dealt with when you set out to ruin me.'

Lucio's eyes narrowed in sharp and angry protest. 'I did no such thing. Business is business.'

'But you didn't like to think someone had a product that could afford you an even healthier bank balance. Is that what you do, go around buying up other people's ideas? Offering them huge sums of money and then making millions for yourself?'

Lucio shook his head angrily. 'What gives you the idea that money is the most important thing in my life?'

'Isn't it?' she countered. 'Wasn't that the reason you gave me for not wanting to get married?'

'I wanted security.' Lucio's eyes were dark and fiery as if he couldn't understand her reasoning. 'I don't think that's a bad thing.'

'But then you much wanted more,' she taunted. 'It's never-ending, isn't it? Instead of being happy with enough to live on you—'

Her words were abruptly cut off by Lucio's mouth claiming hers. His kiss was hot and hungry and promised a night of passion, though why that idea should shoot into her head she didn't know.

'Enough of that sort of talk,' he growled.

Kirstie's first impulse was to push him away but she found that she had neither the strength nor the will-power. It was a night made for lovers. The velvety sky laced with diamonds watched over them. The pines protected them, and the water in the pool lapped gently and appreciatively like a silent audience.

Her mouth relaxed and welcomed his and, feeling her response, Lucio drew in a sharp breath and urged her to her feet. She was held firm against his hard, exciting body, his essential maleness drugging her senses, while his mouth and tongue continued to assault and thrill.

Every ounce of tension went out of her and when his hands moved to cup her bottom, pulling her hard against him, making her intensely aware of his raging need, she wriggled uncontrollably. All those years ago Lucio had been an exciting, innovative lover. What was he like now? What had experience taught him?

And did she really want to find out? Allowing Lucio to make love to her wasn't in her plan of things. It could lead only to a second phase of destruction. So why, then, was she returning his kiss with an abandonment that would make him think that she was once again a willing partner?

Her heart pounded like a mad thing beneath his hot and hungry onslaught and Kirstie knew that she ought to call a halt before her whole world ran out of control. The thought that they might end up in bed both dismayed and thrilled her at the same time.

Lucio apparently had the same thought because she was suddenly set free, left to stumble away from him and reach out for support. Her head spun with dizzying speed and Lucio's harsh voice barely reached into her senses.

'That was incredibly stupid of me,' he muttered.

Kirstie didn't answer. What was there to say? She had been as guilty as he.

'You're such a damned attractive woman, Kirstie.'

But he had never been attracted enough to marry her! Nothing had changed. He wanted her body but not her love. 'I'm going to bed,' she declared firmly, hoping her shaking legs would carry her.

Lucio frowned. 'You don't have to do that; the night's still young.'

And there was enough of it left for him to assault her again. It was a risk she dared not take. She was far too susceptible. His touch, the disturbing male scent of him, even simply looking at him, sent her senses spinning out of control. It was devastating to think that he could still have this impact on her after all these years.

Her only hope of salvation was to keep out of his way, not get into any more potentially dangerous situations. In future she would retire when Becky did, if that was what it took to keep him away from her.

'I think I do have to,' she retorted. 'Letting you kiss me was a mistake, a huge mistake. Don't get the impression that I will ever let you repeat it.'

Lucio's eyes were as hard and dismissive as they had been soft and suggestive a few minutes ago, and an eyebrow rose questioningly. 'Actually I gained the impression that you enjoyed it as much as me. But you're right,' he went on before she could say anything to the contrary, even though she had opened her mouth to do so, 'we don't want to carry on an affair in front of our daughter. How unhappy would that make her?'

His sarcasm cut into Kirstie like a knife. 'You swine!' she cried. 'I'm quite sure you didn't have Becky in mind when you kissed me. You just thought you'd try it on; see if you still had the magic power.'

'And do I?' he asked, a sudden amused light in his dark eyes. 'Actually you needn't answer that. I already know. Nothing has changed, has it, Kirstie?' His velvety voice deepened suggestively. 'You're still on fire for me. You can deny it all you like but curled inside that beautiful body of yours is a tigress waiting to be released. That very same tigress I set free all those years ago. Maybe now isn't the time to free you again, but one day, Kirstie, one day soon…'

Kirstie's breath caught in her throat. 'Is that a threat or a promise?' She wanted to rain her fists on his chest, she wanted to tell him he was wrong, but dammit, he wasn't. He was so right, so very, very right. One kiss was all it had taken to make her realise that sexually she was still as attracted to him as she had ever been. And if he should touch her again, kiss her again, there would be nothing she could do to stop him. In fact her breathing had not yet steadied.

When she had insisted on coming along with Becky it was to protect her daughter; she hadn't realised what a dangerous situation she would be putting herself in.

Lucio smiled disarmingly, knowing how uncomfortable she felt. Even his eyes looked amused. 'It's whatever you want it to be, my passionate friend.'

'I want,' she retorted, 'for you to leave me alone. All you have to do is get to know your daughter; that's what this holiday's all about. It's not about you and me; in fact, there is no you and me.'

A well-shaped dark brow rose. 'Is that so?'

She wanted it to be but she couldn't confirm it. With each second that passed her body was growing treacherously weaker. With one last disdainful look in his direction she spun on her heel and headed indoors.

'Sweet dreams,' he called after her, and Kirstie thought she heard him laugh but she couldn't be certain. Damn the man, he was so sure of himself, so confident that he had her exactly where he wanted her. It would be up to her to prove him wrong.

Sleep didn't come easily; she slept on and off for a few minutes at a time, and during each short nap she dreamed about Lucio. In one dream she was in his bed, they were married and had twin boys who had each crawled in to join them, spoiling their fun. In another they were having a marathon lovemaking session, trying out many different positions.

Every dream was about Lucio making love to her and each time she woke she was drenched with sweat, her heart beating wildly as though it had really happened. It was madness. It was unbelievable. One kiss had turned her mind and sent her body into a fever of excitement.

Over breakfast the next morning, much to her relief, Lucio was coolly indifferent. Whether it was because Becky was present, or because she had told him to keep away from her, she didn't know. Whatever, she welcomed it. On the other hand it distressed her to see Becky looking from one to the other, clearly wishing they would kiss and make up.

If only her daughter knew what kissing Lucio had done to her!

During the days that followed he made no attempt to kiss her again, or even touch her, though several times she found him watching her, even when he was talking to Becky. And when their eyes met a *frisson* of awareness tingled through her.

It was good to see that he and his daughter were getting on so well together, though. Considering he was a bachelor he seemed to know instinctively how to treat her. Which was good because Becky, along with thousands of other teenagers, was at the stage when she thought she was an adult and could do anything adults did. Kirstie had had several disputes with her recently.

But whatever Lucio said Becky did. Whether it was because it was a new thing, or whether it was because he was the male role model she'd always wanted and she looked up to him, Kirstie wasn't sure. But whatever, she enjoyed seeing them so happy in each other's company. It did make her wonder, though, what it would be like when they went back home; when Lucio was no longer a part of Becky's life for twenty-four hours each day.

Would her daughter pine for the father she had only just met? Would she blame her mother for keeping them apart all these years? Would they be as happy as before, or would Becky be dissatisfied now that she'd had a taste of something far different? Only time would give her the answers.

The hot weather drained their energy and they spent hours every day in the pool. Sometimes Kirstie would swim with Lucio and Becky, on other occasions she would be content to sit in the shade and watch. Then there were times when they'd all go walking in the surrounding countryside, Lucio impressing them by his knowledge of the area.

The wildlife was truly magnificent and sometimes they would see lizards scurrying out of the way as they approached. It was a whole new experience and Kirstie, despite the fact that she didn't want to be here, enjoyed every minute.

Occasionally, when Becky and Lucio went riding, Kirstie would have the house to herself. These were her favourite moments, when she could do whatever she liked without fear of Lucio's knowing eyes watching her every move. He was waiting, she felt sure, for the moment to present itself when he could kiss her again. Because she had given herself away, because he knew that he could take her whenever he wanted, he was content to play the waiting game.

It didn't do much for her nerves. That was why she liked it when she was on her own. Lucio sometimes suggested that she and Becky might like to ride together but she always refused, saying, 'I'll be all right. You two need to spend as much time in each other's company as you can.'

She was actually scared of horses, though she didn't tell him that. When Becky had first shown an interest in riding she'd had a go herself, but an untrained groom had put her on a far too spirited horse and she'd ended up being thrown. She was bruised but not seriously hurt, but it had put her off riding for life.

Conchetta, a girl in the village, looked after Lucio's horses and brought them up to the villa whenever he needed them. Thor was a black, highly spirited stallion, and Kirstie's heart rose into her mouth at the thought that Lucio might expect Becky to ride him. But no, Thor was Lucio's horse; he was probably the only man capable of handling him, she thought as Conchetta struggled to keep control. Becky's mount was Venus, a more sedate chestnut mare.

It amused Kirstie to see that Conchetta fancied herself in love with Lucio. She was probably about eighteen and her big brown eyes followed him everywhere. Not that Lucio seemed to notice. He was so used to half the female population fawning over him that it amused rather than intrigued him—at least that was Kirstie's interpretation.

Occasionally Conchetta and Becky went riding together, and when they did she and Lucio would swim or explore, sometimes going to the village to replenish supplies. But he never kissed her again.

'Don't you ever get fed up of it here?' she asked on one occasion when they were hiking up to a series of waterfalls that was by far her favourite walk. 'Aren't you anxious to get back to running your company?'

'When I have you here?' he asked with a mocking lift of a brow. 'And my beautiful daughter? My life has changed. My priorities are different. And at the moment my priorities are making you—and Rebecca—happy.'

It was the slight pause before he said Rebecca that worried Kirstie. Was he suggesting that she, not his daughter, was his main concern? It didn't make her feel good. In fact it unnerved her, just as she was beginning to feel a little more settled. Sexual tension suddenly simmered between them like a time bomb waiting to go off.

It was the hottest day so far and when they finally reached the falls Kirstie forgot her emotions and began to run. 'I'm going under. I'm so hot I could melt.' She was wearing shorts and a T-shirt and didn't mind them getting wet because she knew they'd dry in no time.

She kicked off her sandals and trod carefully over the rock face towards the largest of the falls. And she laughed out loud as she stepped beneath the teeming crystal-clear water. She flung her arms wide and upturned her face, her eyes closed, concentrating totally on the sensation of deliciously cold water taking the heat out of her skin.

When a pair of strong arms slid around her waist and pulled her back against a pulsing hard body she gave a cry of dismay. She'd had no warning of Lucio's approach, hadn't expected him to touch her like this. She had known he would join her—he would have been a fool not to—but if he thought she was inviting love play he was sorely mistaken.

'Get away from me, Lucio,' she cried, dashing the water out of her eyes and flashing the full purple glare of her anger in his direction.

He laughed, a deeply satisfied laugh that told her he had no intention of moving. 'You must have known this moment would come,' he warned, his arms tightening as she struggled to free herself. 'It's been building up ever since I kissed you. You've been driving me crazy, Kirstie, don't you know that? Now is the time for fulfilment.'

CHAPTER EIGHT

LUCIO couldn't explain what had prompted him to sneak up on Kirstie; he only knew that some private demon had taken hold and he was powerless to stop it. It hadn't been in his plan of things when they set off today, but when she stood there like a flying angel his heart had thudded into overdrive and he was beside her in less time than it took to even think about it. And now, beneath his hand, he could feel her heart pumping unsteadily too.

Over the last few days Kirstie had been driving him crazy. He'd made a pledge with himself not to touch her because he knew, after that last kiss, that it could ruin everything. She would most definitely take offence and could quite easily say that enough was enough and fly her daughter back to England.

And he didn't want that. The main reason for this holiday was for him to get to know Rebecca and he was enjoying it, more than he'd ever imagined. She was such a delightful girl. But more importantly he was enjoying getting to know Kirstie all over again.

She had matured so beautifully, was so graceful and elegant. Her auburn hair was longer than it had used to be, and he loved it when she wore it loose. She'd tied it in a pony-tail when they set off but now it had escaped its band and flowed over her shoulders in a silken cascade. And her stunning amethyst eyes never ceased to thrill him. Such an unusual colour, so exotic, so everything! He wanted to look into them for ever more.

And he was being fanciful. He had women galore chasing after him. Why did he want this one woman in particular, especially as he was still so damned angry with her? She belonged to the past; he'd lived without her for over fifteen years. She was going to be a part of his life because of Becky, but that was all. It would be wrong to want anything else of her.

The trouble was she inflamed his senses to such an extent that he couldn't think straight. And he had leapt into action the instant he saw her poised as though she was ready to take flight.

In the north-east of England, on the approach to Tyneside, had been erected a giant steel sculpture, a landmark depicting an angel with wide-open arms ready to greet visitors from any direction. And this is what Kirstie had reminded him of. She had been inviting him into her arms.

And he had taken instant advantage.

Not stopped to think of the consequences.

And now it was too late because already his blood was boiling and his male hormones were working overtime.

The moment had come, realised Kirstie. Already Lucio was turning her in his arms, his dark eyes, impervious to the water cascading over them, hot and hungry, full of passion and desire, and fixed unblinkingly on her face. Here, beneath the waterfall, he was going to make love to her.

Did she fight or did she relax and enjoy? Was it inevitable? Had she known all along that this moment would come and when it did she would be powerless to resist? The answer had to be yes. Lucio had kept her in a constant state of expectation and readiness during the last few days. Each time he had looked at her there was promise in his eyes and her body had zinged with excitement.

Had he woken up this morning and thought, today is the day? Is that why he had brought her up here? He knew she loved it. She loved the wildness of the mountain, the majesty of it, the spectacular falls that never failed to surprise and amaze when they came into view. It was an emotional experience.

Just as feeling Lucio's hard body against hers induced a very different kind of emotion. A powerful longing to feel him once again inside her! Not until this red-hot moment had she realised how much she craved him. He was torture to her soul. The one man she had truly loved. Could she ever love him again? Forgive him? She didn't have the answers, but what she did have was a very strong need. Sense and sensibility didn't enter into it. She wanted Lucio as much as he wanted her.

His eyes burned with an intense light that scared as much as excited her and she was aware of his chest heaving as his breathing grew ragged and desperate. He touched a finger to her lips, stroking, inciting, watching every expression that crossed her face. She was giving herself away, she knew that; she couldn't help it.

He was taking things slowly, excruciatingly slowly, and contrarily Kirstie felt desire building up inside her with the speed of a force-nine gale, and she wondered whether it would reach such a pitch that she would climax before he was anywhere near ready himself.

She closed her eyes, unable to look at him any longer, her head sinking back, the tip of her tongue peeping out to lick his finger, to invite it into her mouth, where she could suck and taste and hunger for more of what he had to offer.

When he moved his hand away she felt bereft and was about to protest, until she felt his fingers at her waist. Every part of her body pulsed hotly when he lifted her T-shirt and willingly she held her arms above her head. Her bra swiftly followed suit. He turned her so that her back was once again against him, his hands cupping the heaviness of her breasts, thumbs and fingers pinching and tweaking her sensitised nipples, his mouth nuzzling her neck at the same time, sending her mindless with desire.

Then he turned her to face him and his mouth took the place of his fingers, sucking first one hungry nipple into his mouth and then the other, grazing with his teeth, nipping and nibbling until Kirstie felt she was going out of her mind.

She could feel him hot and hard against her and a longing so great flooded her groin that she cried out in anguish. 'Lucio, make love to me.'

'All in good time, my darling,' he murmured. 'Why rush the greatest pleasure life has ever invented?'

He continued to torment and incite, to kiss and touch, to suck and bite, driving her further and further over the edge. It had been good before but now it was a hundred times better. No, not a hundred, a thousand! Lucio was doing incredible things, making her lose her mind and her will-power. The whole of her body belonged to him. He could do whatever he liked, take whatever he liked, so long as he satisfied this raging need.

His fingers were on the button of her waistband next, flicking it expertly undone, dragging down the zip with slow, unhurried movements. Why was he doing this when her mind screamed for him to rip the rest of her clothes off and touch her where it mattered most?

And all the time gallons of silky-smooth water poured over

their shoulders. If she opened her eyes she could see the intense blue of the sky and the dazzling rays of the sun, the green of the trees below and the sandy colour of the soil. And each of the colours was diffracted and diffused by the dancing waters. It was magical and beautiful and helped make this moment extra-special.

Finally she stood completely naked, but before he touched her Lucio began to unbutton his shirt. Kirstie couldn't allow that. He had undressed her; it was her turn to undress him. She had done it before but never beneath a waterfall, and never feeling as deeply aroused as she did now.

Her fingers trembled as she took over, and when Lucio circled his arms around her, stroking her back and her bottom in increasingly sensual movements Kirstie felt as if it was taking for ever. It was difficult when his shirt was so wet, when her fingers were all thumbs, and when her emotions were all over the place.

But Lucio was in no rush; he was prepared to wait for however long it took. He was playing her spine at the moment like a skilled pianist, his fingers running down each vertebra in a pagan rhythm.

Kirstie had never thought about her spine being a sensitive part of her body, but what he was doing to her sent waves of deepest need undulating through her. Up and down he went, slowly and suggestively, and all the time she was still trying to undress him. How the hell did he think she could concentrate?

The clip on his trousers was easy, and the zip fell smoothly downwards. Tugging them off his hips was a different matter. The wet cotton clung to him like a second skin and in the end Lucio had to help her.

When he finally stood proud and tall and as naked as the day he was born he cupped her bottom with both hands, and pulled her against him. Kirstie drew in a swift breath of need and pleasure and squeezed her hand down between them to hold him. He was big and hard and his skin was velvety soft, and she wanted him inside her. But Lucio was still in no hurry.

'Later, sweetheart; it's your turn first,' and he removed her hand. 'I'd forgotten how good you feel,' he groaned as he continued his exploration of her body.

Perhaps he was afraid he'd lose control too soon, thought Kirstie, and she didn't really mind because he was touching her most private of places now, making her squirm with pleasure, increasing her hunger, causing her to mew and moan and grip his shoulders so tightly that her nails drew blood.

He brought her to the brink and then stopped. Not once but several times and Kirstie felt as though she was going to pass out, so deep was her arousal.

'You're incredible, Kirstie,' he muttered against her mouth as his tongue ravaged her senses in an entirely different way. 'I can remember how eager you always were to make love, always ready to try something new, but you were never as hot and passionate as you are now. Maybe it's because you're in a hot Latin country? Or maybe it's because you've missed me so much?' An eyebrow rose as he waited for her answer.

Kirstie didn't give him one. She couldn't. She didn't even begin to understand herself. 'I want you to make love to me,' she whispered through a chokingly tight throat.

'And I want to make love to you, my darling, if you're quite sure it's what you want?'

Kirstie nodded, her eyes huge and powerful on his.

She hadn't realised, until Lucio took her hand and led her through the water, that behind the fall was a cave. Or maybe she had noticed but it hadn't registered. It was cool and shadowy and damp but it didn't matter. The walls were smooth, as was the floor, and Lucio backed her up against a wall.

So aroused was she, so heated her body, that she didn't even feel that it was cold and hard. Her senses were attuned to Lucio only, to the feelings that were riding high between them. His eyes met her eyes, both pairs darkly passionate, both desperate for release from the hunger that had smouldered in their souls ever since they had got here.

To begin with he kissed her. It started off as a gentle kiss but in no time it turned into a hard, hungry kiss, both of them eager to taste and explore, to demand and accept, and before she knew it he was preparing himself to enter her.

'You are ready for this?' he asked again hoarsely.

'I'm ready,' she husked. In fact she would die if he didn't do something about it soon.

With iron-strong arms he lifted her against him and Kirstie linked her legs behind his hips, urging herself forward to take him in. It was erotic and exciting and sensual and unrestrained, and they came together in an explosion as wild and untamed as the mountain itself.

Lucio was sure that the contractions that racked his body would go on for ever, and he could hear himself groaning like an animal in pain. He still held Kirstie in an iron-like grip, though she had dropped her feet to the ground, and he felt the waves of intense pleasure that rocked her body the same as his.

It took several long minutes for their breathing to return to something like normal and the heat to leave their bodies. 'Are you OK?' he asked gently.

She nodded. 'I feel different. Do I look it?'

'Absolutely. You radiate a serene kind of beauty,' he said.

'Everything about you has softened and warmed and I've never seen you more lovely.'

Although they were both dry, Kirstie realised to her dismay that their clothes were still heaped beneath the waterfall. They had been so desperate to make love that she hadn't even considered tossing them out. 'What are we going to do about our clothes?' she asked, not that she really wanted to get dressed again; she wanted Lucio to make love to her over and over.

But that was the insane part of her mind. In reality she knew that it had been a foolish mistake, one she would regret once she came to her senses. Nevertheless it had been an out-of-this-world experience.

'We have two choices,' he told her. 'We can put them on and let the sun dry them on our bodies. Or we can lay them out to dry while we...' He didn't need to finish his sentence.

Fresh rivers of heat swam through Kirstie's limbs. Yes, please, she wanted to scream, but sanity wouldn't let her. 'I think we should wear them,' she announced primly.

Lucio shrugged. 'The choice is yours.'

So amidst much hilarity they pulled on their soaking wet clothes and then made their way slowly back down the mountainside. By the time they reached the villa they were dry.

Even though they didn't make love again it was the beginning of a new stage in their relationship. Becky claimed a lot of Lucio's time and Kirstie could see him getting more and more enamoured with this lovely girl who was his daughter and sometimes, when she heard them talking about the future, she had a sinking feeling in her heart. What if Lucio was trying to take Becky off her?

No, that was nonsense; he couldn't be. He didn't have time in his life for a teenage daughter. She was imagining things.

In fact she was probably jealous because he was spending more time with Becky than he was with her.

But at least she and Lucio were friends now rather than enemies and even Becky commented on it. 'It's good to see you and Dad getting on so well together, Mum,' she said one morning over breakfast.

Lucio had been called to answer an urgent phone call from his Barcelona office. His face had gone black with annoyance and he'd not hesitated to tell whoever was on the other end that he'd left strict instructions that he was only to be disturbed under exceptional circumstances.

Kirstie actually thought he'd done very well. She had expected to find an office in his villa. A computer at the very least! Instead there was nothing, although she guessed it wasn't often that he shut himself away from work completely. For all she knew he could have a laptop in his bedroom, where he could work in the middle of the night without anyone being any the wiser.

'I guess we are,' agreed Kirstie. 'Though don't get your hopes too high. We shall never be more than friends.' Inside she could feel herself blushing. Every night in bed she reran their spectacular lovemaking session and knew that she wanted more of the same. But it wasn't the answer. This was but a short interim period in their lives. Once it was over they would go back to their individual lifestyles.

They both had businesses to run; neither of them had time for the other. Lucio particularly. If he'd been the marrying kind he'd have settled down long before now. He enjoyed what he did; he liked the hard work, the challenges, the passing parade of girls. At this point in her thoughts Kirstie's lips tightened. She was one in a long line; she'd best remember that.

Although they hadn't taken precautions up at the waterfall,

Kirstie wasn't concerned that she might be pregnant because she knew that it was the wrong time of her monthly cycle. Another time, though, she might not be so lucky and she needed to remember that. She had let herself get carried away with her spectacularly explosive emotions.

It was hard to believe that she could let herself get into such a state when Lucio had treated her so badly. And there was no doubt that she was confusing love and desire. One minute she doubted that she'd ever loved him, and the next, like in the heat of passion, she was confident that she had loved him once. It was all too baffling.

'That's a shame, Mum,' said Becky. 'I'd love nothing more than for us to be a proper family. You've no idea what it was like at school saying I hadn't got a father, that I didn't even know who he was.'

Kirstie put her hand on top of her daughter's, swallowing a sudden lump in her throat. 'I'm so sorry, darling. I had no idea how tormented you were.'

'It wasn't something I could talk about,' said Becky with a wry smile. 'But things are looking up now. I'm happier than I've ever been, and at least I've found my dad and I'll be able to spend time with him. Do you think we'll ever get to see his other place in Spain?'

'I'm not sure, sweetheart. I don't know what Lucio's plans are.'

That evening, after Becky had gone to bed, Lucio and Kirstie sat outside watching the moon glide slowly across a midnight-purple sky. Little sounds caught her attention; a distant dog barking, a slithering in the undergrowth, a night bird calling. Lucio's heart beating! It was a perfect night for lovers, she thought, her pulses quickening.

Lucio's eyes had made love to her every day. He had kept

her in a permanent state of expectation and, sitting here now, she was sorely tempted to touch his hand, to show him that she wanted something more.

And then he said, in a voice as regretful as her thoughts, 'I have to go to Barcelona tomorrow. I'm sorry, it cannot be avoided.'

'You don't have to apologise,' said Kirstie softly. 'I realise that work comes first.' In fact she was relieved. Her thoughts had been in danger of running away with themselves.

She must never forget the way he had brushed her off all those years ago, would do so again if she dared to suggest a more permanent relationship. He was a virile male and she'd been here for him when he needed a woman. It was as simple as that. If she'd had any other ideas she could forget them.

'Becky and I have had a lovely holiday. And I too have work to go back to.'

'I'm not suggesting that you go home,' he said at once, a frown tugging his thick dark brows together. 'I want you both to come to Barcelona with me. In fact—' he half turned in his seat towards her and took her hand into his '—I hadn't meant to ask you this so soon, but my hand is being forced. Kirstie, I want you to marry me.'

CHAPTER NINE

KIRSTIE'S heart beat painfully fast. A proposal of marriage was the very last thing she had expected. 'Why?' she asked bluntly, unable to think of anything else to say. She certainly couldn't say yes, not after the way her thoughts had been processing the situation. And in her opinion Lucio must have an ulterior motive.

'Why does any man ask a woman to marry him?' he responded, sepia eyes questioning now.

'Usually because he loves her,' she retorted. 'But that's not your reason. I've seen no evidence whatsoever that you're in love with me. You might want my body but that's about all.'

Lucio heaved a sigh and his eyes were sad as he looked at her in the moonlight. 'You're right. I was thinking about Rebecca. I heard what she said to you earlier, about not even knowing who her father was. I want to right that wrong.'

'And you'd marry me for that reason alone?' she asked in disbelief.

'I think it would work,' he said. 'We're still attracted to each other. That hasn't changed in fifteen years.'

'But what has changed,' insisted Kirstie, 'is how I feel about you. I wanted to marry you once, Lucio; you know that.

I wanted it more than anything. But I've changed since then. You've changed. It wouldn't work.'

'So you're saying no?' Dark eyes hardened and narrowed on her face.

She nodded. 'I'm saying no,' and she tugged her hand away from his.

Lucio drew in a swift and angry breath and bounced to his feet. 'Perhaps you need to think it over, Kirstie. I thought you'd be pleased, if only for Rebecca's sake. You're going to make her one very disappointed girl when she finds out.'

'You'd do that?' she asked heatedly, getting up too and glaring fiercely. 'You'd tell Becky I've turned you down? What sort of monster are you?' Her heart drummed painfully against her breastbone and her eyes shot sparks of fire into his. She couldn't believe she was hearing him correctly, or even that this was the same man who had made love to her so beautifully.

'One who cares for the daughter he fathered,' he riposted. 'Maybe you decided to keep her in ignorance of me for fifteen years but I'm not so hard-hearted. I want us to become a proper family, one Rebecca can be proud of.'

'You mean you're thinking of your own reputation?' she questioned harshly. 'If it should get out that you have a teenage daughter it wouldn't be very good for your image, would it? But if you were married to the mother then it would make all the difference. It doesn't matter that you're not in love with me or I with you; it's yourself you're selfishly thinking about.'

And with that she walked away.

Kirstie was stunned; everything inside her had gone numb. Would Lucio really be prepared to marry her in order to give Becky the father she so badly wanted? He would marry a woman he had never loved? It didn't sound like the sort of thing Lucio would do.

She went to bed still puzzling over it and woke the next morning with it still on her mind. She hadn't needed time to think over her answer, though. It remained the same. What was the point in marrying a man for all the wrong reasons? Becky would be happy, she knew that; her daughter would be delirious. But it wasn't the solution. She couldn't marry him for that reason alone.

Sex might be good between them, yes, but how long would that last? How soon before he got tired of her and looked out for another pretty girl to bed? Marrying Lucio would be a recipe for disaster and she wasn't prepared to take the risk.

She would be willing to let him see Becky as often as he wanted—which she knew wouldn't be too frequent because of his work commitments—but other than that she had no desire to commit to anything.

Liar! claimed a little voice inside her. But she ignored it. It was pure lust that drove her where Lucio was concerned and no way was she going to get married on that basis.

Over breakfast Lucio announced to Becky that they were going to Barcelona.

'That's excellent news,' she said with a big grin. 'I really wanted to see your other house. I was asking Mum about it yesterday.'

'And what did she say?'

'She didn't know what your plans were.'

'My plan,' he said, 'was to stay here for as long as I could. You and I have so much catching up to do, Rebecca. But unfortunately urgent business calls and, rather than leave you and your mother here, I thought I'd take you with me.'

More than anything Kirstie wanted to return to England. Lucio's proposal worried her because she knew that, if he said anything to Becky about it, her daughter would nag at her to say yes. In fact Becky would be the happiest girl in the world and the choice would be taken from her—because how could she let her daughter down?

After breakfast a car came to pick them up and at the airport his plane was waiting to fly them to Barcelona. She had actually thought they were going to drive all the way and had been surprised, but not excited like Becky, when they boarded his plane. The pleasure she had felt in such luxury the last time was gone. She was being manipulated into a situation she did not want but could not get out of.

Becky chatted constantly to her father but Kirstie sat quietly, looking out of the window, deep in her worried thoughts. From time to time she saw Lucio looking at her, a faint frown lining his brow, but then his daughter would claim his attention again and he had no chance to speak to her, not on a personal level.

As far as Kirstie was concerned, there was nothing to talk about. She had made her decision and if he couldn't accept it, then it was too bad. However, she had the sneakiest feeling that he would use the strong physical attraction between them to get what he wanted. And lord knew, it would be so easy!

Therefore, in the short time it took them to get from one airport to the other, she packed her emotions into a tight bundle and hid them away in the deepest recesses of her heart, swearing never to let Lucio see them again.

Another waiting car whisked them to his home on the outskirts of Barcelona—a huge, terracotta-coloured villa built on different levels, with a gated entrance opened only by a key fob. It had arches and balconies entwined with bougainvillaea, and wide patios with tubs of vivid red geraniums. It looked welcoming and inviting, but Kirstie was in no mood to be impressed.

Once he had dropped them off and introduced them to his

housekeeper Lucio left. 'I don't know when I'll be back,' he announced, 'but you'll be well looked after. Marietta will show you to your rooms.'

It was not until he had disappeared in a trail of dust from the speeding car that Kirstie breathed a sigh of relief.

'I can't believe my dad owns all this,' said Becky. 'Three properties. How awesome is that?'

'I guess he has nothing else to spend his money on,' said Kirstie bitterly.

'Mum!'

'I'm sorry; I didn't want to come here, that's all. I'd much rather have gone home and made sure everything's OK there.'

'Weren't you curious?'

'Not really.'

'You still don't like Dad very much, do you? What happened? You were getting on so well.'

We made love, that's what happened!

And he asked me to marry him!

'I'm sorry; it's a long story. Maybe I'll tell you about it some time.'

'Like when I'm grown up!' exclaimed Becky angrily. 'I *am* grown up, Mum; why don't you realise that?'

'Some things are private,' she told her quietly, and began to follow the waiting Marietta.

The bedrooms were spacious and impressive and delightfully cool, with balconies overlooking an Olympic-sized swimming pool. One more thing for Becky to enthuse over, thought Kirstie miserably.

After they'd unpacked, refusing Marietta's offer to send someone to help, Becky, as Kirstie had expected, headed for the pool. She tried to encourage her mum to join her but

Kirstie was in no mood for swimming. She wasn't in the mood for anything if the truth were known, except to go home.

She wandered around the huge villa, wondering anew why a man should choose to live alone in such a place. How much time did he spend here, for instance? Was it a matter of having the money so only the biggest and best would do? His mansion in England had astonished her, but now this! It simply didn't make sense as far as she was concerned.

She'd enjoyed his mountain retreat; that was much more in proportion for a single man. Even then he'd had three bedrooms! He evidently entertained a lot, and she didn't need to be a genius to know which sex his guests would be. Or was she being unnecessarily cruel?

Perhaps she was bitter because he'd never wanted to marry her? And now, because she'd introduced him to his daughter, she was once again a part of his life. And this time he did want to marry her. But for all the wrong reasons!

Her mind was in turmoil as she wandered around the villa, peeking into rooms, coming to a full stop when she found Lucio's bedroom. It was the only masculine room in the whole place. Ultra-modern in black, grey and bottle-green. It was minimalist in the extreme and there was not one personal item that could tie it to Lucio, but instinctively she knew that it was his.

She wandered inside, stroking her hand over the grey bedcover, opening a wardrobe to see a neat row of jackets and trousers and shirts. In the adjoining bathroom his toiletries were stowed away behind mirrored cabinets. It looked unused, which wasn't surprising, she supposed, since he hadn't been here for a while.

How much time, she wondered again, did he actually spend

here? Was it worth having all this? But it was what the rich and famous did. Houses in many different countries! She wasn't impressed.

Eventually she wandered outside to explore the grounds and found a separate, smaller detached property tucked away at the side of the house. She presumed it was where the housekeeper lived and for some reason her feet took her in its direction.

It was a lovely, charming place and one where she would have been much happier herself. Perhaps it wasn't the housekeeper's? Perhaps it was used for guests. And if so, why couldn't she and Becky live there?

As Kirstie stood and watched the door opened and an elderly lady dressed all in black with her white hair fixed in a bun at her nape came towards her. It took Kirstie a second or two to realise who she was.

Lucio's mother!

She'd met her in England when she first started going out with Lucio and the woman hadn't attempted to hide her dislike of her. And it didn't look as though her opinion had changed over the years.

'Lucio, he tell me you are coming here,' were her first words. 'He also tell me about his daughter—the secret you have kept all these years. How could you do this to my boy?'

Bonita Masterton had dark, penetrating eyes, cold, condemning eyes, and they were fixed firmly on Kirstie's face. She was a small woman in her late sixties but what she lacked in stature she more than made up for in spirit and mind.

With her hands on her ample hips she stood in battle mode before Kirstie. 'Do you have nothing to say for yourself?'

'I think,' said Kirstie slowly, trying to pick her words with care because she knew how easy it would be to antagonise this arrogant woman, 'I think that your son is as much to blame. He did not want me. He made that very clear.' Thinking about it now, she realised it was probably his mother who had laid down the poison and told him to get rid of her.

'But you did not tell him about the baby. That is a sin.' Stark accusation shone from Lucio's mother's beady black eyes, and her voice rose in passion. 'A sin in the eyes of man and God.'

A cold shiver ran down Kirstie's spine and she wished Lucio had warned her that his mother lived here. 'Do you really think Lucio would have welcomed the news when he was so intent on building a career for himself?' countered Kirstie.

'Pah! When is a career worth more than bringing up your own child? It is my regret I had only one son. But I looked forward to grandchildren. And look what you have done. You have deprived not only my son, but me also.'

'I'm sorry you feel that way,' said Kirstie. 'But I did what I thought was right. Lucio would have hated me for ever if I'd turned up on his doorstep announcing I was pregnant. I did it for him.'

'Nonsense! You didn't do it for him; you did it out of spite.'

Kirstie struggled to keep her voice calm. 'I did it for Lucio's sake, because I knew how much he wanted to become a success in the business world. How could he have done that with a wife and child to look after? It might seem a callous thing to you, but I can assure you—'

'Enough!' spat the older woman. 'I want no more of these lies. Where is this granddaughter of mine? I want to meet her. I want to see what sort of a child you have produced without a father in her life. Children do not have the same respect for their parents as they used to. If Lucio had been—'

'Becky is a very well brought-up girl.' It was Kirstie's turn to interrupt Bonita. She was furious that Lucio's mother should cast such slurs on her parenting skills.

'Becky? Lucio say her name is Rebecca.'

'Becky is short for Rebecca, and she prefers it. She's swimming at the moment. I'll go and fetch her.'

'No need, I come,' declared Bonita imperiously.

And together, in silence, they walked the short distance to the pool.

Becky was swimming away from them and they stood and watched, waiting for her to turn. Her crawl was strong and fluid and her ambition was to swim in the Olympics. This pool must be heaven to her, thought Kirstie, realising, to her dismay, that it would be a pity to take her away from all of this.

'She is a good swimmer,' said Bonita.

Kirstie nodded.

'She take after her father.'

'Maybe,' she answered with a shrug.

'You swim too?'

'Yes, but I'm not a strong swimmer like Becky.'

'Therefore she take after Lucio.' The woman said it proudly and assertively and Kirstie didn't argue. There was no point. Bonita Masterton was an indomitable character, unlike Lucio's father, who was a mild-mannered Englishman, rarely interfering in his wife's arguments. Kirstie had got on well with him.

She recalled the first time they had met. Lucio had taken her to his parents' house and his mother had looked her up and down and come to the instant decision that she was not good for her son. 'You are too young and too pretty,' she had said when they were alone. 'You will stop Lucio becoming a success. He will have his head in the clouds instead of focusing on what he has to do. I want you to finish with him.'

Kirstie hadn't argued with her—she'd been too young and

intimidated at seventeen—but on the other hand she'd had no intention of doing what Bonita asked. It was ironic that the woman had now changed her tune. She must have been tremendously relieved when their affair had ended but now, because she had discovered that she had a fifteen-year-old granddaughter and had been denied seeing her grow up, she still cast Kirstie as the villain.

When Becky reached the other end of the pool she hauled herself out, and upon seeing her mother came walking towards her. 'I love this pool, Mum. It's the best.'

Kirstie smiled her pleasure, but her stomach was churning at the thought of introducing her daughter to this difficult woman. 'Becky, I'd like you to meet your—er—grandmother.' It crucified her to say the word because she really didn't want her daughter hurt. On the other hand, she couldn't stop them getting to know one another. It was Becky's right. She needed to make up her own mind about Bonita.

Becky stared, clearly taken aback, and Bonita looked at her too. For several long seconds they studied each other and then Becky smiled. 'I didn't know you lived here. Dad never said I was going to meet you.' And she held out her hand.

The woman didn't hesitate; she took it between both of hers, already showing her far more affection than she had ever shown Kirstie. 'It is good to meet you. I am sad that I did not know about you before.'

'I am sad too,' said Becky, much to Kirstie's surprise. 'I often wondered who my dad was but I never thought about his parents. Do I have a grandfather too?'

Bonita nodded. 'Would you like to come and meet him?'

'Yes, please,' said Becky eagerly and looked at Kirstie, as if asking whether she would join them.

Kirstie dragged up what she hoped was a happy smile, and together the three of them headed for the smaller house.

'Why didn't you tell me about her?' Becky whispered, hanging back as Bonita entered in front of them.

'Because I didn't know she lived here,' said Kirstie. 'And to be honest I never got on with her when I knew her in England.'

'She seems OK to me,' said Becky. 'I'm so excited about finding a whole new family.'

Indoors Bonita introduced Becky to her husband. 'George, your granddaughter wants to meet you.'

'My granddaughter.' There were tears in his eyes as he spoke. 'I thought I was destined never to have one. Come closer, child; let me look at you.'

Kirstie was concerned to see how old and ill George looked. She remembered him as a tall, virile man, and she had always imagined Lucio looking very much like his father when he grew older. But George was bent and grey now, with deep lines of pain scored in his face. In the corner of the room was a wheelchair.

Becky went willingly to him, putting her arms around his neck and kissing his cheek. 'Hello,' she said nervously.

He smiled and took one of her hands into his, much as his wife had done earlier. Kirstie wondered whether she ought to leave Becky with them for a while so they could get to know one another. Then George held out his hand to her too. 'It's good to see you again, Kirstie. You haven't changed one bit; you're still as beautiful as ever. And you have a beautiful daughter too. Thank you for bringing her to see us.'

Bonita, on the other hand, didn't look in the least grateful. In fact she glared hostilely and Kirstie decided to make her exit.

CHAPTER TEN

IT WAS well past lunchtime but Kirstie didn't feel hungry, even though Marietta had prepared a platter of ham and cheeses. 'Maybe later,' she had said. Her mind was too full of Bonita's vitriolic words where Becky was concerned, and, coming on top of Lucio's suggestion of marriage, it had thrown her mind into turmoil.

She lay down on the bed and closed her eyes, trying to shut out her muddled thoughts, but it was a sheer impossibility. They went round and round like a merry-go-round and her biggest wish was that she had never contacted Lucio. She was bringing nothing but heartache on herself.

Suddenly she sensed that she was not alone. She snapped her eyes open and saw Lucio standing looking down at her. 'What are you doing here?' she asked, sitting bolt upright and staring at him.

'I live here,' he answered with a faint, amused lift to the corners of his mouth.

'I mean, what are you doing in my room?' she tossed back. There was nothing funny in him entering without permission. And she most certainly hadn't expected him back yet.

'I came to find you.'

'Why?'

'The house was empty. I discovered Rebecca getting to know my parents, and I—'

'Why didn't you tell me they lived here too?' cut in Kirstie fiercely. 'You know your mother never approved of me. You could have given me some warning.'

'My mother never approved of you, past tense. Things are different now.'

'Because of Becky?' she yelled. 'Don't you believe it. She tore a strip off me for keeping you all in ignorance.' But if she had expected any sympathy from Lucio she didn't get it.

'And you think you don't deserve it? God only knows how angry I am with you for denying me my daughter's formative years.'

Kirstie closed her eyes and breathed out deeply through her nose. So they were all against her. In that case, what was she doing here? 'You're lucky I got in touch with you in the first place,' she fumed, jumping to her feet and standing right in front of him. 'And if all I'm going to get from you and your mother is verbal abuse then I shall deny you any rights to see Becky again.'

Lucio's eyes sparked fury and she could almost feel the electricity crackling between them. 'You cannot do that,' he raged. 'The courts won't allow it. And have no fear, I will take you to court if you try to keep Rebecca from me.'

Kirstie knew that he would. And he would win. It was no use letting her temper get the better of her where this man was concerned. But neither was she going to be beaten into submission. She had her own sense of values and Lucio was not going to take them from her.

'This is a pointless conversation,' she muttered. 'Why are you really here?'

An eyebrow quirked. 'Isn't it obvious? We have unfinished business. And I thought that, with Rebecca out of the way, now would be a good time to talk.'

Lucio had been so sure that Kirstie would agree to marry him that it had come as a shock when she said no. In fact, he had been damned angry. He had made her the best offer she would ever have. It couldn't have been much fun bringing Rebecca up on her own, and now more than ever the girl needed a father's firm hand.

He had friends with teenage daughters and knew what a handful they could be. Although he had to admit that Rebecca seemed to be a very well-adjusted young lady. He couldn't imagine her getting into trouble. She was well-mannered and pleasant and intelligent, and she'd told him that she wanted to be an occupational therapist, which had impressed him immensely.

But apart from Rebecca needing a father, Kirstie needed a man in her life too. And up there in the mountains she had shown him that he could be just that man. Making love to her had reawakened everything he'd ever felt and he knew that she too had experienced a similar rebirth. So what was it that she still held against him? Was she still bearing a grudge? Or was she afraid? Afraid of the way her body reacted to his? Afraid to show feelings after all this time? Was it pride that held her back?

It was a pity he'd been called away because they didn't have the same privacy here as they'd had in his mountain villa. With his father's ailing health he had insisted on his parents coming to live with him, building a separate annexe especially for that purpose.

'You can talk all you like,' said Kirstie, her amethyst eyes flaring hotly. 'I gave you my answer and I have no intention of changing it.'

Lord, she looked so beautiful that he wanted to roll her back on the bed and make love to her. Not once, but several times. She sent his testosterone levels sky-high simply by flashing those wide, gorgeous eyes. He drew in a deep breath and let it go slowly.

How he wanted her!

He wanted Kirstie to be his wife and one way or another he intended to achieve it.

'Why?' he asked. 'When we make perfect love together?'

'Marriage isn't all about sex,' she riposted. 'There has to be a union of minds as well as bodies. And I'm afraid my mind will never be on the same wavelength as yours.'

'Meaning?' he asked with a frown, although he thought he knew what she was talking about. It always came down to money, and the way he had rejected her so that he could achieve his ambition. Maybe he'd gone the wrong way about it; he had thought a lot of her, maybe he'd even loved her, but marrying her would have meant shelving plans he'd had for many years.

What he hadn't expected was that she would walk out of his life. He had thought they could go on being lovers. And he certainly wasn't going to make the same mistake again. This time he was not going to let her go.

'Meaning,' she said with great exaggeration, 'that I don't have pound signs as brain signals. I'm not obsessed with money the way you are. If we'd met again now and you were penniless, then yes, I'd have agreed to marry you.'

'Which is the most stupid thing I've ever heard,' he roared, except that somewhere in the back of his mind came the thought that she must love him to have said that. And if she did, what was the difference between marrying a rich man or marrying a poor man? What exactly was it that she'd got against money?

He enjoyed his comfortable lifestyle, never having to worry

whether he could pay his bills, like his parents had in the early years of their marriage. He wasn't extravagant; at least he didn't think so, though he knew Kirstie did. He paid his employees well; he looked after his mother and father; he gave money away to charity. What was wrong with any of that?

The only thing missing in his life was a wife!

And he also knew that Kirstie wasn't exactly living on the bread line either. Her little company was doing very well. If he'd known, when he failed in his bid for that clever piece of software she'd created, that Kirstie was the author, he'd have been in touch with her then. Together they could have conquered the world.

'Maybe I am stupid,' she said, 'but I'm happy that way. Can you honestly tell me that you've been happy living a single lifestyle, bedding women but not marrying any of them? Most men are settled down with a family at your age. Your mother was hoping for lots of grandchildren. She's very disappointed in you.'

'So she keeps telling me. Maybe you and I could help make some of her dreams come true?'

'In *your* dreams, Lucio,' she tossed icily. 'I'm getting a little fed up of this conversation. Would you mind going? I want to shower.'

He was going nowhere until he'd got what he wanted. 'Actually, yes, I would,' he answered, marvelling at how even his voice was when what he really wanted to do was shake some sense into her. 'There's still something we need to discuss.'

Kirstie tilted her chin, her amethyst eyes wide and bold and beautiful. Lord, a man could drown in them. 'Marriage is totally out of the question,' she said haughtily. 'What do I need to say to convince you of it?'

'I want my daughter.'

* * *

Kirstie's heart ran icily cold. What Lucio wanted Lucio usually got! That was the sort of man he had turned into. All powerful, believing that money could buy him anything. Except that in this instance money didn't enter into it. He could not buy his daughter.

And he knew it! That was why he was suggesting marriage. Not because he had feelings for her, not because he loved her, but because he wanted Becky! The fact that sex was good between them was a secondary factor. A bonus!

She glared at him coldly. 'You *want* Becky! You make her sound like she's something you can buy. You cannot buy love or people. Becky would love me to marry you, I know that, but she's star-struck because you've got loads of money. She doesn't know the true you. The sort of man who would never be there for her; who thinks more of his business affairs than he does his nearest and dearest. At least I had the sense to work from home so that I would never have to leave her.'

'But you didn't have the sense, or the decency, to tell me you were pregnant,' he shot back, dark eyes accusing. 'You're no saint yourself, Kirstie.'

A faint stab of guilt penetrated her heart. It was true; she had shied away from telling him. But her reasons had been altruistic. She really had thought that he would be incensed, that he would blame her. And she had wanted to spare him. Her life would have been hell if he hadn't been able to achieve his lifetime's ambition.

'I actually believe I did you a favour, Lucio.'

'That isn't the issue,' he declared fiercely. 'We're talking about the here and now.'

Of course it wasn't the issue, because he knew damn well

that she was right. 'I am not marrying you simply to give Becky the benefit of a father she does not need.'

'Of course she needs me,' he claimed hotly. 'Wasn't that the sole reason you came to see me? You cannot change your tune now, Kirstie; it's far too late.'

He was backing her into a corner! Kirstie closed her eyes and then wished she hadn't when she felt his warm breath on her face and his mouth close over hers. But if he thought physical persuasion was the answer then he needed to think again. She had made up her mind. She was not going to marry Lucio Masterton. Ever!

His kiss was warm and slow and intoxicating. It melted her bones and sent tiny shock waves vibrating through every nerve and vein. Don't let him do this, warned an inner voice. Break away now, before it's too late.

But it was too late already. An arm slid around her waist and bound her to him, while his other hand cupped the back of her head and made sure there was no escape. His tongue tasted and plundered and Kirstie felt herself going quickly mindless with desire. Lucio knew exactly how to arouse her deepest emotions, but if he thought he could get through to her this way—he was—he…

Her thoughts ran out of steam. Excitement took over. She entwined her tongue with his; she tasted the electrifying maleness of him, she felt the surge of his desire against her and urged herself even closer, her hips gyrating in a mindless rhythm. He was not going to get his way—she had made up her mind on that, and she was not going to marry him simply because he thought it would be the correct thing to do; but taking what he had to offer seemed like the right thing at this very moment.

That was what her body told her, but it was warring with

her mind. This was insanity; it was giving him all the wrong signals, and if Lucio kept her in this excitable state she would end up doing what she did not want to do.

Nevertheless it took every ounce of will-power to slide her hands up between them to press against the hard, throbbing wall of his chest and push him away. At least that was her intention. It did not work out exactly like that because his hands caught her hands and held them there, and his mouth continued to seduce and devastate until Kirstie felt herself weakening all over again, until all she wanted was for this man to make love to her. He had already drugged her senses to such an extent that sanity no longer entered into the equation.

Slowly he edged her backwards until she felt the bed behind her knees. Her heart pounded and she knew that this was the point of no return. At the same time she heard Becky calling out to her. 'Mum, where are you?'

Reality swiftly returned. Lucio released her but she saw that he was smiling confidently. 'I'm up here, darling.' He'd had her exactly where he wanted her and if he'd done it once he knew that he could do it again. He didn't mind the interruption.

Becky came to a swift halt when she saw Lucio in her mother's bedroom, but there was nothing on either of their faces to suggest that they had been doing anything other than talking. At least, Kirstie hoped not. There was certainly nothing in Lucio's expression to give away the fact that he had been about to make love to her. Which made her wonder how much of it had been real, and how much a sneaky plan designed to get his own way.

She was grateful to Becky for interrupting them and she made a vow there and then that she would never let him get that close again.

'I didn't know you were back, Dad. *Abuelita* wants to

take me shopping. Will that be OK?' She looked at them both expectantly.

'It's fine by me,' said Lucio.

But Kirstie frowned. *'Abuelita?'*

'Grandma,' informed Lucio.

Grandma! She was calling Lucio's mother grandma already! 'Why would she want to take you shopping?' she asked sharply. She was cross with Lucio's mother for even suggesting it. In her opinion this was another member of the Masterton family trying to buy her daughter with money.

Becky's mouth turned down at the corners and Kirstie could see an argument ensuing.

'Let her go,' said Lucio, reading the signals on her face. 'It's important for her to get to know her new grandmother.'

'She doesn't need to have money spent on her to get to know her,' declared Kirstie tetchily. 'It sounds like your mother's trying to buy her friendship, the same as you!'

Lucio's eyes grew stony, but his voice was even. 'I don't think we should be having this conversation in front of Rebecca.'

Kirstie knew he was right so she dragged in a deep breath and nodded to her daughter. 'OK, you can go, but—' She had been about to say 'but don't ask for anything', then changed her mind. 'Enjoy yourself.'

'I will, Mum. Thank you.' Her dark eyes, so like her father's, shone like diamonds, and she skipped back out of the room.

'Why is it,' asked Kirstie before Lucio could speak, 'that your family think that spending money on someone will buy their love?'

'That is not the case, and you're wrong to think that,' he answered tersely. 'It gives me, us, great pleasure. Our reward is in seeing the response, the joy, the excitement. It's not about buying someone's love, as you so crudely put it.'

'Hmph!' snorted Kirstie disbelievingly, but she left it at that.

'Now, where were we?' he asked.

Kirstie backed away with horror in her eyes. 'You're unbelievable! Do you really think I'd carry on where we left off? I'm glad Becky interrupted us; I can see now that I was out of my mind.'

'Not out of your mind, my beautiful Kirstie; simply following the dictates of your heart.'

'My heart?' she echoed loudly. 'It was my treacherous body that let me down.'

'Body? Heart?' he scorned. 'They're both the same. You can't resist me, Kirstie, and you know it.'

He sounded so confident that she could have hit him. 'And you think that because my body is dangerously weak where you're concerned that it naturally follows that I'd be willing to marry you? Think again, Lucio.'

'I've done nothing but think about you since you came back into my life,' he answered, smiling faintly.

'Because you want to lay claim to your daughter!' she accused, eyes shining hotly. 'I'm a means to an end, that's all.' And she was fed up with constantly going over the same thing. Why wouldn't he, couldn't he, take no for an answer and let them get on with their lives? Except that life would never be the same again!

Becky would for ever be pestering her about her father, wanting to see him again, wanting to spend time with him. An explosion had gone off beneath their feet and shifted the axis of their world. It was up to her to steady it again and ensure that her daughter came to no harm.

Kirstie crossed to the door and stood to one side, holding the handle, indicating that it was time for him to leave. 'This conversation is getting us nowhere and I really would like that shower,' she announced tersely. She did not expect him to go, in fact she felt sure that he would attempt to kiss her again.

And when he came to a halt mere inches in front of her, so close in fact that she could smell the devastating cologne that he always wore, so close that she could see a faint dark rim round the already dark brown of his eyes, she felt a tremor begin to build up inside her.

Lucio had become a threatening male animal. He made the hairs stand up on the back of her neck whenever he was close. She feared for her life, and the life of her child! An exaggeration, she knew, but fear was a big part of her thoughts. She could so easily submit herself to him. He had proved to her that she was not immune to his charm. One tiny step on her part and it would be all over.

He ran the back of a gentle finger down her cheek and smiled. 'We have the house to ourselves. Rebecca has just given us a golden opportunity. Why not leave your shower until later?' His voice was gruff with emotion and it churned Kirstie's stomach.

'If you're suggesting we make love then forget it,' she told him tightly.

'Why, when you enjoy it so much?'

He was enjoying this conversation. He knew that he held her in the palm of his hand and that if he should so much as touch her she would be his.

Kirstie squirmed. Everything inside her scrunched into a tight ball and she tried to glare at him. Almost impossible when what she actually wanted to do was fling her arms around his neck and kiss him. No, she didn't, she told her inner self. Yes, you do, it replied. Why not say to hell with the consequences and go for it?

But how could she do that? How could she forfeit her comfortable lifestyle to live with Lucio and suffer when he was absent? None of it made sense. He only wanted her because of Becky. She must keep reminding herself of that. And he had only ever wanted her as a bed partner; otherwise he would have come after her when she walked out on him all those years ago. It was all he wanted her for now. No real commitment, no love, nothing but a marriage sham. Something to save face when he finally had to admit to the world that he had a fifteen-year-old daughter.

'Maybe I do enjoy it,' she told him, 'but it's not the answer. You're sorely mistaken, Lucio, if you think I'll ever marry you.'

His face hardened; his eyes became as glacial as an iceberg. 'And that's your final answer, is it?'

'My final answer,' she agreed.

'In that case I shall simply have to think up some other way to gain possession of my daughter.' And with that parting shot he swung on his heel and left the room.

CHAPTER ELEVEN

KIRSTIE felt as though she'd been punched in the solar plexus; she was left gasping for air, staring at the closed door, wanting to go after Lucio but knowing it would do no good. He had most definitely meant what he'd said about taking Becky off her and she was scared. He was quite capable of doing it. The big question was, how?

Becky had grown so fond of her father that she could easily be persuaded to spend time with him, and once he had her in his power he would never let her go. Kirstie rued the day she'd phoned him.

She had thought at the time that she was doing the right thing, and now everything had turned around and she was in grave danger. Little did Becky know what sort of a power freak he was. If Lucio set his mind on something he didn't give in until he'd got it. His initial aim had been total success, a zillion in the bank and a lifestyle to go with it. He had ruthlessly achieved that ambition. And now he had a new objective: her daughter.

For the rest of the afternoon, until Becky came back from her shopping expedition, Kirstie didn't leave her room. Her mind ran riot trying to look for a way out. Maybe she ought to emigrate to the other side of the world? Do a disappearing act with Becky.

She didn't really want to leave her comfortable home, though. She was happy there, and she had her business to run. Why should she let Lucio Masterton scare her away? He couldn't take Becky against her will. And if she warned her daughter of the situation then Becky would be on her guard too.

Or would Becky enjoy living with her father? Would she jump at the opportunity? Kirstie didn't like to think so. His wealth had impressed her. It hadn't turned her head—yet. But who knew what the future would bring?

Her head thumped incessantly and she took a couple of tablets and threw herself down on the bed. When the door opened she looked across in alarm, thinking it was Lucio come to taunt her again.

'Hey, Mum, what are you doing? Don't you feel well? I've had a fabulous time. Barcelona has the most wonderful shops and *Abuelita* bought me a fantastic top. Wait till you see it.'

Kirstie sprang to her feet. 'I wish you hadn't let her buy you anything.'

'Why?' Disappointment filled Becky's eyes.

'I don't want her to think that I can't afford to clothe you.'

'Don't be silly, Mum. She won't think that. She's adorable.'

Adorable wasn't an adjective Kirstie would use to describe Lucio's mother. On the other hand, Becky hadn't seen the side of her that Kirstie had.

'So what's wrong, Mum? Why were you lying down? And where's Dad? I thought the house was empty. I thought you two had gone off somewhere together.'

'I've no idea where your father is,' answered Kirstie tersely. 'And I have a pounding headache.'

'Have you fallen out with him again? You didn't look too happy when I came up earlier.'

Kirstie shrugged. 'We've had words, yes.' She saw no point in lying because the atmosphere between them would be palpable in the extreme.

'What about?'

'Nothing you need concern yourself about,' she lied.

'You said that the last time. I want to know what's going on.'

'And I have no intention of telling you, Becky. It's personal.' How could she tell her daughter that her father was planning to kidnap her? It would ruin her happiness; it would ruin her image of him. Either that, or she wouldn't believe her anyway. It was best left unsaid. This was something she needed to sort out herself.

'You don't tell me *anything,*' cried Becky and stamped from the room.

Kirstie put her hand to her head. Her temples throbbed. In fact her whole body ached with anger and disappointment. She needed a long walk in the fresh air and how she wished they were back in the mountains. A climb up to the waterfall would be cathartic and she could wash away her headache and her fears and doubts beneath the teeming silver cascade.

She deliberately pushed away all thoughts of Lucio making love to her up there; at least she tried to. But images and feelings returned with a vengeance and she thumped her fists against the door. Why had her world gone suddenly so wrong?

'Mum, are you OK?'

It was Becky. Kirstie had thought she'd gone downstairs again, but apparently she was still in her room and was now feeling concerned for her mother.

'I'm fine,' she called out. 'In fact I think I might go for a walk.'

'Or you could swim with me,' said Becky. 'I'm heading down there now. I'm sure it will do your headache good.'

It sounded a sensible solution. Far better than getting lost in a strange city! 'Perhaps you're right,' she called. 'I'll be down shortly.'

'Make sure you are,' answered her daughter.

Kirstie couldn't help smiling. She'd said this so often to Becky when she'd claimed that she was going to do something later. Her daughter really was growing up.

Actually the swim did her good. Her headache settled into a dull ache and the energy needed to swim several lengths of this giant-sized pool drained away her anger. She was actually beginning to enjoy herself—until Lucio appeared!

He wore black swim shorts and was clearly intent on joining them. His magnificent body, lithe and well-honed, with not an ounce of superfluous fat, captured her eyes. He was clearly of the opinion that being a success in business meant keeping in superb physical condition. He would need to, she supposed, to keep up his strength for the long hours he worked.

Lucio too seemed unable to take his eyes off her. An electric charge ran through her limbs and she damned herself for being so responsive to him. It was madness in the face of the threat he'd made earlier.

There was no sign of it on his face, though. He smiled warmly. 'Do you ladies mind if I join you?'

'Of course we don't,' said Becky before she looked anxiously at her mother.

'Do whatever you like.' Kirstie shrugged dismissively, trying to pretend that she did not care, when in fact she would have liked nothing better than to scream at him to keep away from her daughter.

She saw Becky looking at her worriedly and so she fixed a smile on her lips as he swam towards them.

'Did my mother spoil you?' he asked Becky, surfacing at their sides.

'I wouldn't let her,' said Becky. 'But I enjoyed my time with her, thank you. And I'm sorry my grandfather doesn't get out much. He's a nice man too.'

'You're very generous,' he said. 'My parents were delighted when they found out they had a granddaughter and they want to make up for lost time. You must forgive them if they go a little bit over the top. Especially my mother! She's very excitable, as you've probably found out.'

And determined to castigate her for keeping Becky a secret, thought Kirstie inhospitably. She didn't share her daughter's admiration for her new-found grandmother, and Bonita certainly didn't feel any affection for her either. Becky was the only one welcome into her family.

If Bonita knew of her son's intention to take Becky off her she would throw in her weight as well. Nothing would please her more; that was a fact. It wasn't only Lucio she needed to be wary of, it was his whole family!

'You've gone very quiet, Kirstie.' Lucio touched her arm and his dark, penetrating eyes were gentle on her face. 'Are you all right? Do you still have your headache?'

Kirstie frowned. She hadn't told him that she had a headache.

'I saw it in your eyes earlier. It's why I left you to rest.'

Liar! Kirstie wanted to yell. You knew nothing of the sort. You had one thing in mind when you came to my room. Well, two actually. One was that you wanted to get me into bed. The other was to tell me that, unless I married you, you intended taking Becky off me. And he'd planned to do it in that order. Sweeten her first and then drop his bombshell.

She shivered as she looked into bruising sepia eyes. 'It's almost gone,' she choked out, careful not to overreact in front of their offspring.

He stroked fingers over her forehead, gentle fingers, soothing fingers, and Kirstie closed her eyes. He didn't seem to mind that his daughter was watching them, intrigued. Or was this all for Becky's benefit? Did he want her to think that he and her mother were the best of friends again?

'Mm, that feels good.' The words slipped out and she was annoyed with herself, because even though they were true she didn't want him to know. 'I think maybe you should have been a masseur; you know exactly where to touch to make it better.'

'Indeed I do.' His voice was a low, soft growl, full of innuendo, and Kirstie could feel the blood rushing to her cheeks. What must Becky be thinking? But when she opened her eyes she saw that her daughter had slid silently away and was swimming lazily to the other end of the pool. Her little girl was being tactful!

'Is there anywhere else you'd like me to touch?'

Kirstie found it hard to believe he was acting like this after the parting shot he'd cruelly left her with earlier.

'Like here, for instance?' Beneath the waterline his hand skimmed over her breasts, making her nipples tingle and leap forward in eager anticipation.

'Why are you doing this?' she asked breathlessly, feeling a deep ache in the back of her throat.

'Don't you like it?'

Like it? She loved it! 'You know I do,' she admitted unhappily.

'You cannot resist me, can you?'

'Don't ask me these questions,' she hissed through her

teeth. 'They're pointless. You're using nothing short of emotional blackmail to get your own way.'

'You're wrong,' he said with a smile which suggested innocence but she knew was lethal. 'I'm doing this because I can't resist you. You're a beautiful woman, Kirstie.'

'So you're playing with me?'

'Not in the way you're thinking. There's no reason why we shouldn't have a good love life, even if we don't agree on other things.' As he spoke he tweaked each of her nipples between thumb and forefinger, making her eyes shoot wide and a tiny moue of excitement escape her lips.

And then, before she could even begin to protest, his hand moved swiftly downwards, expert fingers sliding inside the bottom half of her bikini, finding the hot core of her that was already pulsing with pleasure.

She wriggled uncontrollably and had an insane urge to grab him too, but fear that their daughter might come swimming back and catch them stopped her. She wanted to tell Lucio to stop, she wanted to push him away, but again she didn't want to upset Becky by her actions. And Lucio knew this. It was why he was making the most of the situation.

And lord, was he doing it. Every inch of her throbbed with hungry pleasure and she kept urging herself against his hand, feeling herself being brought to the very brink of wild abandonment.

'This is good for you?'

'Mm, yes,' she groaned. 'But if you don't stop this very minute our daughter will find out what you're doing.'

'You're that close?'

'You know I am.'

'Can I come to your bed tonight?'

'Yes!' she cried. *'Yes!'* But then a brief flash of sanity entered her mind. 'No! I mean no. Oh, please, Lucio, stop!' It was so hard not to thrash against him, to give way to the explosive sensations that were building catastrophically inside her. She wanted to grab him and hold him close, to feel his arousal, to reach her climax while he was still holding her. She wanted him to feel her excitement, to be a part of it.

'You really want me to stop?' he asked easily, his fingers encouraging and torturing her red-hot flesh, turning her soul inside out, turning her whole body into a molten state of ecstasy.

'No! Yes! I don't know. Oh, God!' It was too late. She shuddered to a silent climax, though how she managed to stop herself shouting out she did not know. Lucio wrapped his arms around her and held her close, and if Becky was watching them she wouldn't know that her mother had just experienced one of the most fantastic orgasms of her life.

What Kirstie really wanted to do was sink down to the bottom of the pool and lie there, hugging her knees to her chest, letting wave after wave of ecstasy wash over her. Each tiny movement brought fresh sensations and each time she urged herself against him Lucio's arms tightened.

'That was good for you?'

She gave a faint nod, feeling too weak to speak.

'You're fantastic, do you know that?'

Kirstie groaned. 'What I do know is that I haven't the strength to move.'

'No need! We can stand here for as long as you like.'

'Where's Becky?'

'Still at the other end of the pool,' he assured her when he felt her start of alarm. 'She has no idea what's gone on. She's smiling happily. She likes to see us getting on well together. And we are going to get on, for the whole of the rest of her holiday; aren't we?'

Kirstie wasn't sure whether that was a threat or not. But her rosy euphoria hadn't yet gone so she nodded dreamily.

'Good girl!' And he continued to hold her against him, stroking her hair, not letting her go until he felt the strength seep back into her body.

By the time Becky rejoined them Kirstie's body had returned to normal; well, almost. She still felt a rosy glow that she imagined would be with her for most of the day, but outwardly there was no sign of the violent eruptions that had taken place within her.

She felt happier, though, than she had in a long time, pushing out all thoughts of the future and what was going to happen then, taking part in swimming races with Lucio and Becky, never minding when she always came in last. They were like one happy family and she felt sad when Lucio declared that enough was enough.

They each went to their rooms to shower and change and over dinner that evening Lucio was warm and loving and there was nothing at all to show in his behaviour that he had given her an ultimatum.

Kirstie couldn't help wondering whether he would come to her bed later. She knew that she must not let him, that it would be tantamount to letting him have his own way, not only physically but in other directions as well.

Like taking Becky off her!

On the other hand, she knew that she wouldn't have the will-power to stop him. She only had to think about what had happened earlier to experience a tightening of her pelvic muscles and a tingling sensation throughout her whole body. During their meal his eyes had promised her all sorts of pleasures, which she had tried to ignore for her daughter's sake, but, alone in her room later, she knew they would come tumbling back and her body would ache to be held by him.

And it happened just as she had imagined.

She opened her door to his light tap and their eyes met and held and all she could do was step back and allow him to enter. They needed no words. Their bodies were hot for each other and they fell into each other's arms, their mouths meeting and tasting and bruising, and their bodies exploding and melting time and time again as they made frequent love.

It became a nightly ritual after that.

During the day Lucio would spend time with both of them, though there were occasions when he needed to shut himself into his office. He had enjoyed showing it off to Kirstie and she had been duly impressed. Nothing but the latest equipment, most of it designed and manufactured by his own company. It was so high-tech it was surreal and she could imagine that he needed never leave his office chair. At the touch of a button he could be in visual and vocal contact with anybody in any part of the world.

The whole villa was full of high-tech equipment. Everything you could imagine worked by remote control or the touch of a panel button somewhere on one of the walls. Outer doors automatically locked behind you, but were voice-controlled when you wanted to go out.

He had bodyguards too, so discreet that Kirstie had not at first noticed them. A gardener, a window cleaner, a pool attendant! They were all highly trained to look after him and his parents.

It was not the way Kirstie would have liked to live. Wealth brought with it many disadvantages, the major one being that you were a prime target for crime. It did not appeal to her at all.

During each evening, when the three of them ate together,

sometimes joined by Lucio's parents, Lucio was charming and attentive, regaling them with anecdotes about his working life, and Becky clung to his every word. Kirstie couldn't help worrying how this would affect her when they went back to England and their more modest and normal way of life.

Not once did Lucio mention taking Becky off her and Kirstie wondered whether he had changed his mind. Or, a more sobering thought, was he hoping that she would change her mind? That she would miss him so much, miss their explosive love sessions, that she would agree to marry him after all?

It was after dinner one evening, when his mother had joined them, his father having gone to bed early because he wasn't feeling well, that Lucio was called away to the phone. Becky too disappeared. Lucio had installed a computer in her room and she wanted to see if she'd had any emails from her friends in England.

'My son, he tells me that he has asked you to marry him and that you have refused?' said Bonita without preamble.

Kirstie was appalled that Lucio should have confided in his mother. She went cold at the very thought. Bonita was of the old school and was clearly unhappy that he'd fathered a child out of wedlock. But had he really needed to tell her that he'd proposed?

'That's right,' Kirstie agreed reluctantly. 'Lucio didn't ask me because he loved me, he asked me because he wants Becky. What woman in her right mind would agree to marry a man who doesn't love her?'

'Do you love my son?'

It was such a direct question that Kirstie felt swift colour flood her cheeks. She was in love with Lucio the lover, but not with Lucio the man and father. There was no point in loving him. No matter what his mother might think and want,

Lucio had never loved her enough for marriage; not sixteen years ago, not now. His motives were entirely egotistical.

'No, I don't love Lucio,' she answered firmly.

'Then why did you invite yourself back into his life?'

'I did it for Becky's sake!' Kirstie told her crisply. 'She wanted to meet her father.'

'And now?'

'I don't know what you mean.'

'And now you are going to take her away again?'

Kirstie lifted her chin and looked at the woman haughtily. 'I cannot live with a man I do not love.'

'Not for the sake of your child?' shot back Bonita caustically.

'I shall not deny him access.'

'Access? Pah!' declared the older woman. 'You are as selfish now as you ever were. I wish my son had never met you.'

'You think I haven't wished that a thousand times over?' countered Kirstie.

The old woman's eyes narrowed. 'You do not love your daughter?'

'Of course I love Becky,' retorted Kirstie hotly. 'I cannot imagine my life without her.'

'Just as Lucio cannot imagine a life without his daughter either.'

'Has he asked you to plead on his behalf?' queried Kirstie, purple eyes flashing her anger.

Bonita reared up. 'My son, he does not know I am talking to you. He would be very angry. Lucio is a big man; he can stick up for himself.'

'I'm glad you appreciate it,' said Kirstie drily. 'But if you think any interference on your part will help matters, then I'm sorry, but you're wrong. Lucio and I will work this thing out for ourselves.'

'You're not making a very good job of it so far.'

'And how would you know that?' demanded Kirstie.

The woman shrugged. 'I know what I see.'

She had seen them playing happy families, but she hadn't seen them making love throughout the night. Unless—Kirstie felt a cold shiver slide down her spine—unless she had seen them in the pool that day? Discreetly observing them, watching what her son could do to this girl who was playing a much bigger part in their lives than she would have liked. Kirstie's chill was replaced with a fiery heat that spread through each of her limbs until she felt her whole body was on fire.

'You've seen nothing,' she riposted. 'Lucio and I will never see eye to eye.'

'I realise that, and if I am honest I do not want you for a daughter-in-law. But I want my son to be happy, and if marrying you will make him happy then that is what you must do. Without love if necessary.'

Kirstie couldn't believe she was hearing this. It looked as though the whole Masterton family was hedging her into a corner from which there could be no escape. And if she put the option to Becky she knew that her daughter would want her to marry Lucio too.

In fact, Becky would be devastated when the time came for them to leave. She had bonded so well with Lucio that it would break her heart.

'I do not need you to make my plans for me.' Lucio had entered the room on silent feet and his face was enraged as he stood looking down at his mother. 'I can do that very well for myself.'

His mother lifted her shoulders and let them drop again and then muttered something in Spanish before getting to her feet and leaving the room.

'I apologise for my mother,' he said. 'She had no right interfering in our affairs.'

'Mothers care,' informed Kirstie.

'Naturally, but they should know when to hold their tongues. I'm afraid my mother is not very good at that.'

Tell me about it, returned Kirstie beneath her breath. Bonita was the most outspoken woman she'd ever met. It was sometimes difficult to understand why George had married her and, what was more, remained married all these years. He was a lovely man, so quiet and patient, always ready with a kind word and an attentive ear.

She'd gone to see him again the other day when she knew Bonita was out and he'd been so welcoming, so pleased to see her. He'd hugged and kissed her and said he hoped that she was now going to become a permanent part of their lives.

Kirstie couldn't promise him that.

'So exactly what did my mother have to say, apart from proposing to you on my behalf?' Lucio enquired, resuming his seat at the table and gazing straight into Kirstie's eyes.

She felt a quiver of excitement begin in the pit of her stomach; a quiver she knew would turn into raw need if he kept looking at her like this. Sometimes she thought he was seeing into her very soul; that he knew everything she was thinking and feeling.

CHAPTER TWELVE

LUCIO was furious with his mother for speaking to Kirstie about such private matters. Who knew what else she might have said if he hadn't returned? Yes, he thought Rebecca should have a father in her life. Yes, he thought Kirstie should marry him and give their daughter security. But no, he did not think his mother should have interfered in his affairs. And when he saw her next he intended telling her so.

Not tonight, though, while he was reeling with anger. Tonight he needed Kirstie in his bed like never before. Kirstie could make him forget everything. He could sink himself into her body and not remember anyone else existed.

There had been women in his life, but none who could arouse his deepest feelings the way Kirstie did. She drove him mindless with desire. It was as though their bodies were made for each other. Fanciful thinking on his part—not something he was much given to—but the fact remained that she stirred the deepest recesses of his soul. She took it and made it her own and he was willing to give her his all.

He was deeply disappointed that she had refused to marry him; he had meant it when he said he wanted Becky to be a part of his life in future. Having missed the first fifteen years, he wanted time with his daughter now. And if by the end of her stay here Kirstie hadn't changed her mind then he would take matters into his own hands. He was determined on that point.

But maybe he was being premature. If the physical part of their relationship was anything to go by he had high hopes for their future.

'What did your mother have to say?' Kirstie repeated his question but it felt as though her voice was coming from a long way off. And he didn't care whether she answered or not.

And when she got to her feet he groaned and pulled her roughly into his arms. 'To hell with what she said; let's go to bed.' And his mouth joined with hers.

Afterwards, a long time afterwards, when their bodies were warm and soft, when Kirstie's head was nuzzled into his shoulder and his long, strong fingers were lazily stroking her breast, he said, 'I think maybe we should go exploring today. Barcelona's a magnificent city and I've not shown you the sights yet.'

'Mm, I'd like that,' agreed Kirstie. 'Can Becky come too?'

'Naturally. But first,' he said thickly, his sex hormones beginning to stir again, 'I think I should do further explorations on your body.'

It was mid-morning before the three of them finally set off and Lucio was duly proud of this city he'd made his second home. One of his men drove them and then followed a few yards behind as they strolled around the city. At first it made Kirstie feel nervous but after a while she forgot about him and began to enjoy herself.

La Rambla, a long, wide street, made up of five different streets, according to Lucio, ran from one impressive square to another towards the sea and was *the* place to be. It was exciting and vibrant and teemed with people; tourists and locals alike. Streets led off it and back again and there was so much of interest to see. The architecture was second to none, and there was an infinite variety of shops, news kiosks, flower stalls, cafés, and much, much more.

Lucio wanted to take them into an exclusive restaurant for lunch but Kirstie insisted on sitting at one of the pavement cafés simply so that she could people watch. The stream of people was endless, some chatting to their companions and not even noticing their surroundings, others gazing in awe at the majestic buildings, cameras capturing snapshots of the moment.

'Rambla means torrent in Arabic,' Lucio told her as they sipped iced drinks while waiting for their food. 'It flowed here along a sandy gully before it was paved over.'

'It's all so incredible!' breathed Kirstie, her eyes darting here, there and everywhere. Even Becky was impressed.

After their meal they wandered in and out of various museums and galleries and inspected the harbour. Becky wanted to do the shops, though, and, much against Kirstie's wishes, after they had opened again after the siesta, Lucio bought her a whole wardrobe of clothes.

Back at the villa they had a light supper and before Becky went to bed she flung her arms around Lucio's neck and kissed him soundly on the cheek. 'You're the best dad in the whole world. I'm so lucky to have found you.'

Kirstie winced, wondering how cruel it would be to take Becky away from this life of luxury. She wanted none of it for herself, but Becky was different. She had found the father she had craved and a whole new world besides. Kirstie had some very hard thinking to do.

Later, when he came to her room, Lucio asked whether she'd enjoyed her day.

'It was lovely, thank you,' she answered. 'I truly loved every moment of it. But I wish you hadn't spent so much money on Becky. You mustn't spoil her.'

'She's my favourite girl and worth spoiling,' he returned with an insouciant grin. 'Next to you, of course.'

Kirstie had already showered and slipped into a pink silk robe, knowing there was no point in putting anything else on because Lucio always took it off. 'You have a beautiful body; why hide it?' he would say. And he never lost time in taking his own clothes off.

Sometimes they showered together, but tonight, because of their long day, Kirstie had been in desperate need, and, judging by Lucio's crisply curling hair, he had showered too. He smelled totally gorgeous, and when he stood behind her and slipped her robe off her shoulders she sank back against him in ecstasy.

But instead of him touching her, instead of him starting on his tortuous path of seduction, she felt something cold slide around her neck. Then he urged her across the room so that she could see herself in the full-length mirror.

'Oh, Lucio!' she exclaimed. For there around her neck was an elegant gold chain and, nestling in the hollow above her breasts, was the largest cluster of diamonds she had ever seen. It was beautiful and breathtaking, and her fingers wandered upwards to touch and admire.

But then her hand dropped abruptly to her side. 'I can't accept it,' she declared in a tight little voice that sounded nothing like her own. 'I won't have you spending money on me like this. It's bad enough that you spent a fortune on Becky but I guess you have an excuse as she's your daughter. But I am nothing to you and I—'

'You are not nothing, Kirstie,' he riposted, his face grim all of a sudden. He spun her around and looked closely into her amethyst eyes. 'Don't ever think that,' he threatened. And then he kissed her. And the kiss took away every thought of rejection. It filled her whole body with the sweetest sensations, made her realise exactly what she would be missing if she insisted on seeing no more of Lucio once they were back home in England. It suddenly struck her that she couldn't do it. She wanted to be with Lucio for the rest of her life.

Not that she intended telling him yet. The idea was raw and needed to be carefully considered before she made her final, irrevocable decision. But tonight she would wear his necklace with pride, she would allow him into her bed again, and they would make wild and abandoned love as they never had before.

When Kirstie awoke the next morning she was still wearing the necklace. The bed beside her was empty but warm and she smiled contentedly. Lucio always slipped away before Becky came wandering into her room. Not that she would be upset to find Lucio sharing her mother's bed; in fact she would be delighted. But Kirstie had always felt it would be wrong for her daughter to see anything like that when she had no intention of marrying Lucio.

Now it had all changed. She had thought long and hard about it last night after Lucio had fallen asleep, and she realised that she could do worse. Love wasn't the important factor here; giving Becky her father was. And who knew? Love might grow again, the way it had when she'd first met Lucio. Certainly some of the anger she'd felt against him was slowly dissipating.

She went down to breakfast with a smile on her face and hope in her heart, only to find that Lucio had gone out. But he'd left her a note saying that he would be back as soon as he could and that he was throwing a party that evening for Becky's birthday.

'I didn't know he would remember, Mum,' said an excited Becky. 'I was afraid to remind him in case he thought I was angling for another present. He's so generous it's unbelievable. My friends are green with envy.'

Kirstie thought he had forgotten too, even though she had only told him a few days ago. She had bought her daughter a watch that had cost quite a lot of money, but seemed like nothing now, compared to the expense and trouble Lucio was going to. She wished he had told her what he was planning. Who was going to help get everything ready? Poor Marietta would be run off her feet.

But then an army of people arrived and the grounds were transformed with fairy-light grottos and a platform for a pop group that had been hired to play and a dance floor and a marquee for whatever purpose. And then later in the day food and drink arrived, piled into gigantic chiller cabinets that were plugged into sockets already set in the grounds of the villa.

There was still no sign of Lucio but Becky was beside herself with excitement. 'I'm the luckiest girl in the world,' she sang as she danced around the place. 'Do you think he'll invite some young people as well?'

'I'm sure your father has thought of everything,' answered Kirstie crisply.

Becky gave her a strange look but said nothing.

It was almost six before Lucio came home and he looked pleased to see that everything had been set up just as he'd ordered. 'A nice surprise?' he asked.

Kirstie shook her head. 'More like a shock.'

He frowned. 'What does Rebecca think?'

'She's over the moon.'

'So what is the problem?'

'I think the least you could have done was tell me what you'd planned.'

'Why? Don't you like surprises? It's not as if I was asking you to do anything.'

No indeed! Everything had gone like clockwork. She had never seen such perfection, but she couldn't help wondering how much this sort of thing cost. Not that it would matter to Lucio. Money meant nothing to him these days.

She had gone from deciding that she could do no worse than marry him to thinking that he was way out of her league. If this was the sort of event he regularly put on then his life-style wasn't for her.

'Smile and enjoy,' he said. 'I'm going up for a shower. Care to join me?'

Kirstie shook her head.

'Come on, don't sulk.' He touched a finger to her chin, sending a stream of sensation trickling through her veins. 'We mustn't spoil this for Rebecca. Haven't you noticed how happy she is that you and I are getting on so well together? We can't ruin that on her birthday, now, can we?' He bowed his head and touched his lips to hers, and Kirstie felt an explosion of feeling and was lost.

Lucio in this mood could not be resisted.

Kirstie dressed carefully for the party. The aftermath of their lovemaking had left a glow to her skin and an indelible smile on her lips and she virtually danced around the room as she got ready.

She had not brought anything with her that remotely resembled a party outfit but she had a silky black low-necked sun top and a pair of wide-legged floaty black trousers which, when teamed together with a gold belt and gold high-heeled sandals, looked good enough to party in.

She had taken the gold necklace off when she got up that morning, but now she fetched it out of the drawer where she had carefully placed it and was about to fix it round her neck when Lucio came into her room. Only the lightest of taps heralded his entrance but she did not mind. 'Allow me,' he said huskily.

Kirstie was so afraid that he would want to make love to her again that she almost refused. It was definitely not wise to let Lucio touch her because it set off a chain reaction inside her body and there was not a thing she could do about it.

And he knew it!

She watched him in the mirror as he fastened the necklace, total concentration on his devastatingly handsome face. And when he had finished he stood there, his hands gently cupping her breasts, a thumb brushing over the tips, and already exquisite forms of pleasure raced through her, which, considering they had made love such a short time ago, was nothing short of amazing.

Lucio did this to her.

Lucio made her feel all woman.

It would be a crime to let Lucio go.

Her smile almost split her face in two. 'Lucio, we'll never attend the party at this rate.'

And then another tap came on her door and Becky entered. 'Mum, Dad, I'm ready. How do I look?'

She saw nothing wrong in the two of them standing so close together and it made Kirstie wonder whether she had been aware all along that he crept into her room each night.

She turned and appraised her daughter. 'You look stunning, darling.'

'So grown up,' said Lucio in awe.

She was wearing one of the new outfits Lucio had bought

her, and Kirstie guessed that he'd had this party in mind when he had taken their daughter shopping. A strapless cerise dress made her look slender and elegant and much older than her sixteen years. Her dark hair hung loose and she wore very little make-up, just a touch of colour to her lips and a dash of mauve eye-shadow. On her feet was a pair of ridiculously high-heeled shoes.

She was wearing the watch Kirstie had given her that morning and now Lucio fetched a slim package out of his pocket and handed it to her. 'Happy birthday, darling.'

'But Dad, you bought me loads of clothes, and you've organised a party, I don't want anything else.'

Kirstie was proud of her. Her immediate reaction had been one of horror that he was regaling Becky with yet more presents, though she wouldn't have said anything, not until they were alone. And she was pleased that Becky felt the same.

'I insist, Rebecca,' he said now. 'It's not much, just something to remind you of your birthday.'

Not much! Inside the white leather box was a pair of gold earrings with an ornate letter R dangling provocatively. He'd obviously had them specially made and they must have cost the earth—the same as her necklace.

'Oh, Dad, they're beautiful!' exclaimed Becky, giving him a big hug and kiss. 'I'll treasure them for ever. Look, Mum, aren't they just perfect?'

Kirstie forced a smile and nodded. 'They're lovely, darling. You're a very lucky girl. I hope you realise that.'

'I do, I do. I'm going to put them on now,' and she skipped back out of the room.

'You don't approve, do you?' asked Lucio, looking at Kirstie.

'No, I don't,' she answered crossly. 'You shouldn't spend so much on her. It's not good. I've tried to teach her the value of money but you're undoing all that. She'll begin to realise that she can ask and have and that's not right. I've always encouraged her to save up for the things she wants. She's had a bank account since she was little and—'

Lucio held up his hand. 'OK, I get the picture. But surely you can understand my point of view?'

'I understand but I don't agree,' she said with a flash of her amethyst eyes, 'and I don't want you to spoil her any more.'

He didn't promise anything. He drew in a harsh breath instead and said gruffly, 'Have you any idea how gorgeous you look when you're angry, Kirstie? I want that fire inside you to be *for* me, not against me. I want to take you to bed, right now, this very minute.' He gripped her arms so tight that it hurt and his mouth sought hers. 'I want—'

The door burst open and Becky came in with her new earrings in place. 'Look, aren't they—? Oh, I'm sorry. I didn't realise I was disturbing anything.' And then she grinned. 'Carry on; forget me—I'll go down and see if any of the guests have arrived.'

'I guess we should go down too,' said Lucio ruefully. 'It would be wrong of me to let Rebecca cope on her own when she doesn't know anyone. Maybe we'll find time to slip away later.'

He made it sound as though they were carrying on an illicit love affair, thought Kirstie with some amusement. The fact that he came to her bed every single night didn't seem to count. Not that she was complaining. Her heat for him was equally urgent. And already she had forgotten her anger.

He looked amazingly sexy in fitted black jeans and a black short-sleeved shirt, a suitable outfit for a teenager's birthday party, she thought, and was impressed by his consideration.

'Did I tell you that you looked stunning too?' he asked as he tucked her hand into his.

She laughed. 'We're both dressed in black. Do you think I should change?'

'Only if you let me do it,' he growled.

'I don't think we have time for that,' answered Kirstie, knowing full well what would happen if he attempted to undress her.

'Then we'll go as we are,' he announced, and together they left the room and headed downstairs.

They reached the garden in time to greet his first guests, and after that a constant stream of people arrived, young and old alike. Some were friends of his parents, and others were his own friends with their sons and daughters. Becky was in her element, not at all shy, and using the few Spanish words that she had learned to impress. Soon all the youngsters were dancing to the disco and Lucio and Kirstie mingled with the crowd.

Lots of curious looks were sent in her direction and she guessed that tongues were wagging now that Lucio had suddenly produced a sixteen-year-old daughter. Not that he minded. Indeed, he was as proud as punch to show her off. And he was proud to introduce Kirstie too.

The party was in full swing when a late arrival made a grand entrance. She was raven-haired and beautiful and wore a scarlet halter-necked dress slashed right down to her navel, and no jewellery whatsoever. She walked tall and proud and her eyes worked the crowd, looking for one particular person.

That person was Lucio, of that Kirstie was very sure. She did not know why; it was simply that her inbuilt antennae had picked up the signals. He had not yet seen the lady in red; he was talking to a friend of his father's. Kirstie had wandered away from him, watching Becky dancing with a group of boys and girls. They were having a wonderful time and she was grateful to Lucio for doing this for her.

When the newcomer finally saw her quarry her eyes lit up and she called out his name. Lucio turned and a smile lifted his face too. Kirstie continued to watch them. She expected the vision in red to hurry over to him, but no, she stood and waited for Lucio to come to her.

Which he did, never once taking his eyes off her, leaving Kirstie to wonder exactly what the relationship between them was.

CHAPTER THIRTEEN

'THEY make a handsome couple, don't you think?' Kirstie turned and found Lucio's mother standing at her side. 'Lucio has known Simona for many years. I used to think that one day they would get married.'

'And now, do you still wish that?' Kirstie watched as Lucio hugged Simona, kissing her lingeringly on the lips, and it was easy to see that he was very fond of her—and she of him!

'I want my son to be happy, whatever he decides,' answered the older woman diplomatically, but because Kirstie didn't think that discretion was Bonita's forte she was immediately suspicious.

'I thought you wanted him to marry me?'

'It would be best,' came the resigned answer. 'Even though Simona is the one he truly loves.'

Kirstie's heart instantly turned to stone and dropped to the pit of her stomach, where it settled heavily and uncomfortably. The way Simona and Lucio were hugging and kissing confirmed what Bonita had said. And she knew that even though her thoughts had been warming towards the idea of marriage it was now an impossibility.

'Excuse me,' she said to his mother, not wanting to hear

her extol any more virtues of this handsome woman, and she disappeared into the crowd, smiling and passing cheerful greetings with no sign that her world had just collapsed. A few minutes later she felt Lucio's hand warm and heavy on her shoulder. 'Kirstie, there's someone I'd like you to meet.'

Carefully fixing a smile on her lips, even though it killed her to do so, Kirstie turned.

'This is Simona Carrasco, a very old friend of mine. Simona, meet Kirstie Rivers, the mother of my daughter.'

Simona's dark eyes fixed on Kirstie's face unfalteringly, and they sent a message of hatred. The touch of her hand was brief and cool. 'How interesting,' she said in a carefully modulated voice.

Kirstie couldn't even find her voice. She gave a brief smile of acknowledgement and looked daggers at Lucio instead. *The mother of his daughter!* Not his friend, not his lover, but the mother of his daughter. As though she'd done a job for him, producing a child.

In contrast Lucio smiled at her warmly. 'Simona's been on holiday in the West Indies. She only got back today. I didn't expect her to make it tonight.'

And I wish she hadn't, thought Kirstie acidly. She suspected that Simona had come because she'd heard about Becky and her mother and wanted to see them for herself. And she didn't like what she saw, that much was very evident. Her wide dark eyes shot daggers and her scarlet lips turned down in disdain.

'Let's dance,' said Simona, when the music suddenly changed from disco to something slow and romantic. And she took Lucio's hand, dragging him in the direction of the dance floor.

He rolled his eyes and looked apologetically at Kirstie. She forced herself to smile and then turned away because she didn't want to see Simona draping herself over him, or Lucio holding her close and whispering in her ear.

Lucio's father was on the edge of the crowd, watching her, and he beckoned her to join him. 'Come and sit down,' he said, wheeling his chair over to an empty bench far enough away from the music so that they could talk without shouting. 'I see you've met Simona.'

Kirstie nodded, her lips compressed, not wanting to say anything detrimental in case he was as fond of this other woman as his wife was.

'You mustn't take too much notice of her. She's had her sights set on Lucio for a long time but he's not interested.'

It hadn't looked that way to her, thought Kirstie. His eyes had lit up when he saw Simona. And the hug and kiss were certainly not those of a platonic friend.

'He takes her out whenever he's over here,' continued George, 'but there's no more to it than that. Simona lives in hope while he's still single and one of the most eligible bachelors around. It must have been a real shock to her system when she found out about you and Becky.' His eyes twinkled as he looked at her. 'My bet's on you.'

Kirstie put her hand over his. 'Thank you; you're very kind.' And she hadn't the heart to tell him that she didn't think it would ever happen.

'All those wasted years.' He held her hand between his and looked into her face with his watery blue eyes. 'It's sad. Having Becky here reminds me of you all those years ago. So young and full of life—not that you aren't now, mind, but you were so much in love. I wanted you to marry Lucio. I told him off for letting you go. Not that it made any difference. I guess he was too young and ambitious to settle down.'

Kirstie nodded. 'I'm sorry I didn't tell any of you about the baby. I found Lucio's rejection hard to handle and couldn't afford to go through it again. I thought he'd be angry, perhaps even say I got pregnant on purpose.'

'So you bravely brought Becky up on your own. You have my admiration, Kirstie. She's a credit to you.'

'Thank you, George.' Out of the corner of her eye she saw a flash of red disappearing round the other side of the house. And when her eyes scanned the crowd there was no sign of Lucio. Anger rose up inside her. 'Excuse me,' she said, 'I need to go and check on something.'

'That's right,' said George with a slow smile. 'Don't let Simona think she's going to get it all her own way.'

Kirstie grinned, feeling immediately better now that she had the older man's backing. But on her way Becky waylaid her. 'You must come and meet my new friends, Mum.' And it was several long minutes before she could go looking for Lucio.

He was nowhere in sight and she couldn't help suspecting that he had taken Simona up to his room. It hurt like hell to think that he might even at this minute be making passionate love to the lady in red. Never, she thought, wrapping her arms around herself, would she let him touch her again.

Dejectedly she walked back to the party. She caught George's eye across the lawn and shook her head but she didn't go to him. Tears were too near the surface. Tears and anger. Bitterness and regret. It was time she went home.

She wasn't short of company; everyone wanted to speak to her, to find out what sort of a person she was who had borne Lucio a child and kept him in ignorance. Not that they were unfriendly, they were all very nice to her, but always Kirstie had one eye on the lookout.

It seemed like hours but could only have been minutes before she spotted them rejoining the party. Simona looked profoundly satisfied but Lucio's eyes were scanning the crowd, and when he saw Kirstie he headed straight towards her.

'I'm sorry I've been neglecting you,' he said with one of his devastating smiles. 'I needed to get Simona up to date with what's been going on in her absence.'

Kirstie frowned. 'I don't understand.'

'She works for me.'

'I see.' This was entirely unexpected and she swallowed hard. 'What is she? Your personal and private secretary?'

He cocked an eyebrow. 'Do I detect the green eye of jealousy?'

You're damn right you do! But she didn't admit it. She lifted her shoulders instead. 'Not at all. I'm just surprised that you mix business with pleasure. Surely it could have waited?'

'Simona is very conscientious.'

I bet she is, thought Kirstie.

'Are you enjoying yourself?'

'Yes, thank you. Your father says Becky reminds him of me when we first met.'

'Very true,' he agreed. 'Young and wild and free. Why did I ever let you go?'

He would have taken her into his arms but Kirstie dipped away. She could smell Simona's perfume on him and it made her feel sick. If Lucio thought he could get the best of both worlds he was deeply mistaken.

Suddenly the music faded and everyone headed for the tables of food. Kirstie let herself be carried along by the throng and although she knew that she couldn't eat a thing she filled her plate. Simona had claimed Lucio again, she noticed, and so she silently slipped away to her room, dumping the contents of her plate in a bin on the way.

She had been so close to agreeing to marry Lucio that it scared her. He had given no hint that there was another woman in his life. She wanted to believe his story that Simona worked for him and there was nothing more to it than that, but she couldn't. He wouldn't have greeted Simona with a kiss and a hug if that were the case. He was lying. And she hated him for it.

Kirstie sat in her room for a long time before reluctantly accepting that she must rejoin the party. Not that she was being missed. Not by Lucio anyway, or he would have come looking for her. She wasn't even in his thoughts, not while he was with Simona. He was a two-timing bastard and she hated him.

At the top of the stairs she met Simona coming up, alone, a flash of evil in her eyes when she spotted Kirstie. 'The very person I'm looking for,' she trilled in her perfect English.

Kirstie lifted her chin and prepared herself for battle. 'I can't imagine that you and I have anything to say to each other.'

'Believe me, I have plenty to say,' came the swift retort. 'Shall we go to your room?'

'I don't think so.' Kirstie stood that little bit taller. 'Here will do nicely.' She could guess what was coming.

'You do know,' said Simona without preamble, 'that Lucio's in love with me?'

Kirstie lifted fine brows. 'No, I didn't know. Are you sure? Most men love to brag about their love life. Lucio has never mentioned you.'

A faint frown marred the smoothness of Simona's brow but it was gone instantly. 'That's because he's discreet,' she said, her tone deeply defensive. 'But in case you're getting any ideas, you being the *mother of his child*,' she spat the words with derision, 'I think I should warn you that you're wasting your time. Lucio and I were planning to get married before you appeared back on the scene.

'He told me about you, how you begged him to marry you when you weren't much older than your daughter is now. How you've kept his daughter a secret all these years.' Her eloquent dark eyes flashed hostility. 'He hates you for that. He's being nice to you for Rebecca's sake, but he can't wait for you to go back to England and leave him to get on with his life.'

'A life which includes you, I presume?' asked Kirstie coldly, wishing that Lucio hadn't filled this horrid creature in with all the personal details of their life. Her backbone turned to ice, every vein and artery freezing; even her blood had stopped flowing.

She felt like an ice sculpture and wondered whether she would melt and flow away when Simona had finished with her. Or would she remain in this frozen state for ever? She knew that the lady in red was being deliberately spiteful but there had to be some element of truth in what she was saying.

'Yes,' agreed Simona. 'I cannot imagine life without Lucio. Whenever he's in England my heart dies a little, even though we speak to each other every day.'

'And yet you went away on holiday without him.' Kirstie could not hide her scorn. 'Or did some other man comfort you in his absence?'

The briefest flicker in her stunning dark eyes revealed that Kirstie had hit a chord, but there was no sign of it in her voice. 'Why would I need anyone else when I have Lucio? I took advantage of taking some time off while he was in England,' she said with her chin high. 'Lucio even paid for me. He's such a generous man; he buys me gifts all the time.'

And that's why you're hanging on to him, thought Kirstie

in disgust. It was his bank balance that interested her. Simona clearly had a vision of a long life of luxury. And she was afraid that vision was going to be taken away.

Except that Kirstie didn't need any warning. She had seen for herself how attracted Lucio was to this scarlet woman who was almost wearing a dress that was sheer provocation to any man. No wonder he had disappeared into the house with her.

Kirstie touched the diamond necklace at her throat. 'Yes, he is generous, isn't he?' And she felt great pleasure when she saw Simona's frown. 'Now, if you've quite finished I'd like to rejoin the party. Becky must be wondering what's happened to me.'

'Just one moment,' spat Simona, barring her way, her eyes alight with malice. 'My guess is that Rebecca's not really Lucio's daughter, that you're simply claiming she's his because you've found out how very successful he is and you want a share of his fortune.'

Never before had Kirstie felt like hitting another woman as she did now. How she kept her hands to herself she did not know. Nevertheless her eyes shot sharp daggers of hatred. 'Maybe you would lie to get your man, Simona, but it's the last thing I would do.' And, pushing her out of the way, she made her way downstairs, back ramrod straight, chin high, hot colour flaring in her cheeks.

Whether Simona followed she didn't know and she didn't care. The woman was nothing more than a spiteful bitch and if anyone was after Lucio's money she was the one.

'Whoa, what's the hurry?' Lucio's arms caught her as she rushed outside like a demented demon. 'I've been looking for you.'

From somewhere she summoned up a smile. 'Nature called. Where's Becky? Is she still enjoying herself?'

'She's having a ball,' he announced. 'Most of the youngsters speak English, which is good, although Rebecca's showing an amazing flair for Spanish.'

Kirstie nodded. 'She can already speak French and knows a little German.' And why were they talking like this when what she really wanted to do was tell him she was ready to go home and he was welcome to Simona?

Inside she was still fuming over the Spanish woman's insinuation that she was trying to trap Lucio into marriage. It was preposterous. Simona herself was the one trying to snare him. And the revealing red dress was part of her plan.

Why was it that men were so weak? A pretty face and a voluptuous figure and they were lost. A shiver ran down her spine and Lucio was instantly attentive. 'Are you all right, Kirstie? You look flushed.' He touched his fingers to her brow. 'You're hot. Do you feel unwell?'

'As a matter of fact I feel absolutely rotten,' she retorted. 'But I don't want to spoil Becky's party so I'd prefer it if you said nothing.'

'Can I get you anything? An aspirin, a glass of water?'

'No, thanks,' she snapped. 'But I would like to be left alone.' She failed to see the hurt in his eyes.

'Perhaps you're right; perhaps you should sit quietly somewhere. There's my father over there; perhaps you'd like to keep him company?'

Kirstie nodded and then wished she hadn't because it made her head spin.

Lucio tucked her hand through his arm and led her over to his parent. 'Kirstie's not feeling well. Will you keep your eye on her for a while? There's someone I need to speak to.'

'Always work,' muttered his father, but Lucio didn't hear.

'He's the one who should be sitting with you,' he declared. 'But never mind, you sit here and tell me all about it.'

'That woman's wicked,' she claimed, watching Lucio as he walked away. He had the narrowest hips and the neatest bottom; even in the state she was in she couldn't help noticing. He was altogether the most gorgeous man she'd ever met—and also the most lethal. He was a two-timing manipulator and she wished with all her heart that she had never gone out with him in the first place.

'Who? Simona?'

'Yes.'

'She got to you?'

'You could say that. Do you know what she accused me of? Lying about Becky being Lucio's daughter. She said I was after his money. Lord, I felt like hitting her.'

George chuckled and laid a hand on her knee. 'That I would like to see. She's a nasty piece of work, without a doubt. But you shouldn't let her get to you. You're the one Lucio loves, even though he may not know it.'

Kirstie huffed her disbelief.

But George shook his head and went on, 'He's like all red-blooded males—he has an eye for a pretty girl. I enjoy looking at Simona myself,' he added with a chuckle, 'especially in that dress. But make no bones about it, Lucio only has eyes for you.'

Kirstie privately thought that his father was deluding himself. It was only Becky Lucio loved and wanted.

'So what else did the sniping Simona have to say?' asked George when she remained silent.

Some of the fire was leaving her and her cheeks didn't feel so hot, but she was still angry with Simona for playing the temptress and Lucio for falling prey to her charm. 'I really don't want to talk about her any more,' said Kirstie.

'Very well, tell me about yourself instead. What have you been doing all these years, apart from bringing up my very delightful granddaughter, of course? Look at her.' His attention was instantly taken up by Becky and his question forgotten.

Becky was in a circle of boys, all hanging on to her every word. She had certainly been made welcome in their midst and Kirstie's heart burst with pride. Becky was never shy in new company, but this was a different country as well and she was behaving as though she had known them all her life.

With her dark hair and her father's sepia eyes Becky looked very much at home. Suddenly she caught her mother's eye and waved. Kirstie waved back. At least someone was happy.

'She's a delightful girl and a credit to you. I hope you're not going to take her away from us again?'

Kirstie smiled and shook her head. 'She has school, of course, but there are always holidays. I think I'd have a job keeping her away. She adores Lucio already. He'd be happy for her to live with him.'

'But Becky would only be happy if you were there too,' he added intuitively.

Kirstie nodded.

He patted her knee. 'Who knows what the future might bring?'

Kirstie was glad when the party ended. One by one the guests drifted away until there was only Simona left. And it looked as though she had no intention of leaving until she and Lucio were finally alone.

Bonita and George had returned to their house, George with an assuring wink when he bade Kirstie goodnight.

Becky had worn herself out and had gone up to her room with a smile on her face and a great big thank you to Lucio for arranging the party.

Kirstie had wanted to help clear away but Lucio wouldn't hear of it. 'I pay people to do that job. You still look out of sorts, Kirstie; I think you should go to bed too.'

And leave you with Simona!

Out of the corner of her eye she saw the lady in red's satisfied smile.

CHAPTER FOURTEEN

LUCIO was concerned about Kirstie. One minute she'd been fine and the next she'd been consumed by a raging fever. He'd wanted to insist she go to bed, but he knew she wouldn't do that while the party was in full swing. She wanted to keep her eye on her precious daughter, and who could blame her? He felt the same himself, even though he'd only known Rebecca for such a short space of time.

He'd not been expecting Simona back today and wondered how she had heard about the party. That she was in love with him he was fully aware, but he was not in love with her. She was a beautiful and proud addition to any man's arm, but she was also doggedly persistent. He had told her many times that he would never marry her and yet still she hung around.

She hadn't been pleased to find out that he had a sixteen-year-old daughter. How had that happened? she'd wanted to know. Are you sure she's yours? Why didn't Kirstie ever tell you? And so the questions had rained.

He always tried to let her down gently because he was genuinely fond of her, but she'd tested his patience to the limit this evening and he wished she hadn't hung on to the very end. He would have liked to make sure that Kirstie was all right.

Now he was committed to driving her home. 'My driver

will take you,' he'd said when she asked him, but Simona had pouted prettily and said she wanted him to do it.

When they got to her house she invited him in and it soon became clear that she intended inviting him into her bed as well. It wouldn't be the first time she'd offered herself to Lucio, and probably not the last, but tonight he wanted to get home to Kirstie. He was concerned about her. He hoped she wasn't coming down with something.

'Do you really have to go?' asked Simona softly, draping herself over him, blatantly provocative.

'Yes, I do,' he insisted, putting her from him. 'I want to check on Kirstie; she's not well.'

'She seemed all right to me when I spoke to her,' declared Simona petulantly.

'Maybe she did,' he agreed, wrongly thinking that Simona meant when he had introduced them. 'But she's certainly running a fever and I don't want it getting any worse.'

'Are you going to marry Kirstie?' came the next fully charged question.

'It's a possibility,' he answered carefully.

'Because she's the mother of your child and you feel it's the right thing to do?'

When he paused before answering she went on, 'It wouldn't work. You and Kirstie are poles apart, whereas you and I—' she pouted again and fluttered her long eyelashes '—are perfectly suited.'

'Darling Simona, you know that's not true. How long have we known each other? Too many years to remember. But all we are—all we will ever be—is good friends.' And she knew it. But she wouldn't accept it. It was time he was out of here. '*Buenas noches,*' he said, heading towards the door.

'Lucio!'

He turned and saw tears in Simona's eyes. 'Is this the end?' she asked in a miserable little voice.

He strode back to her and touched her shoulders. 'We will always be friends, you should know that.'

'But I want more.' And she took his hand and slid it inside her dress.

'Make love to me, Lucio,' she pleaded. 'Stay the night; let me have one last night of pleasure with you.'

He would not have been human if he hadn't felt a reaction to this woman and an urge to do as she asked and pump himself into her until he was exhausted.

He had planned to spend tonight in Kirstie's bed, and his body craved fulfilment.

But Simona was not the woman he needed or wanted.

He was in love with Kirstie and no other woman would do. Yes, he was truly in love with her.

'I'm sorry, Simona, I can't do that,' he said, freeing his hand and stepping back.

She was beautiful and curvaceous and sexy and infinitely desirable, but his heart belonged to someone else. There was only one woman in his life now. And one way or another he intended making her his wife.

The siren spat fire. 'You really are going to marry the bitch, aren't you? How do you even know that the brat's yours? You're out of your mind. She's out for what she can get; it's as clear as the nose on my face. You'll see. But when you realise and come crawling back, don't expect me to be waiting. Now *get out*!'

Wrath hath no fury like a woman scorned, thought Lucio as he turned and left the house. He wasn't sorry to be rid of Simona. She'd become a touch too clingy lately. Even if Kirstie hadn't turned up he would never have married her.

On the drive back to his villa Simona was forgotten and his thoughts were with Kirstie. In his haste to be with her he drove well above the speed limit, but when he skidded round a bend and ended up off the road he mentally dressed himself down. You're no good to Kirstie in hospital, he warned.

When he got home he leapt the stairs two at a time and quietly pushed open Kirstie's door. Her curtains were drawn back and in the dim light from the moon he could see that she was asleep. Her face looked pale in the moonlight and when he touched her forehead her temperature was normal. Relief flooded over him.

He was tempted to climb into bed with her, but instead he stood looking at her for goodness knew how long. Maybe a minute, maybe an hour. Enough to reassure him that this was the woman he wanted to spend the rest of his life with. Enough to make him sad that he had once ruthlessly dispelled her. Enough to convince him that Rebecca really was his daughter despite what anyone else said.

Simona hadn't been the only one to suggest that Kirstie might be playing him along, and he had given each one of these doubters short shrift. As far as he was concerned there was no disputing the fact that he was Rebecca's father. There was so much of him in her that anyone with an ounce of sense could see it.

He was so proud of the way she had behaved today. He had feared she might feel awkward and had watched her constantly; ready to move in if he should see any sign of discomfort on her part. But she had not needed him or her mother. She'd had the time of her life and was now contentedly asleep in bed.

He was aware of the fact that Kirstie was worried he might spoil Rebecca—and how much he wanted to! But he would rein in those feelings and respect Kirstie's wishes. That way she would never again be able to accuse him of trying to buy his daughter's love.

Finally he made his way to his own bedroom. How empty it felt after all the nights he had spent with Kirstie. Maybe he should sneak into her bed, give her a pleasant surprise when she woke in the morning. But something told him that this wouldn't be right. Her temperature had felt normal but she might still be feeling under the weather, and if that was the case she wouldn't want him hungry to make love to her.

When Kirstie awoke she reached out to feel for Lucio. The bed beside her was cold and empty. Then she remembered. He had taken Simona home. She had watched from her window as he helped her into his car and her heart had felt heavy.

She had lain awake waiting for him to return but eventually her eyes had closed and she had no idea now whether he had come home or not. If he had it would be the first night he had not slept with her.

Had Simona flaunted her beautiful body and tempted him into bed? Had she wriggled her hips and bared her breasts? Had Simona sated Lucio? Kirstie clapped her hands to her head. She did not want to know.

Lucio was at the breakfast table when she went down, reading the morning newspaper and drinking coffee. An empty plate told her that he had already eaten. And he looked bright and cheerful. Obviously he'd had a good night, she thought bitterly.

'Kirstie, good morning,' he said at once, putting down his paper and smiling. 'How are you? I must say, you look much better.' He stood up and would have pulled her to him except that she turned sharply away.

'I'm fine,' she announced coolly, pulling out a chair and sitting down.

Lucio frowned. 'But something's wrong?'

'Yes,' she said abruptly, 'I want to go home. We've stayed here long enough.'

He sat down again, his brown eyes narrowed and questioning. 'And what's brought this on, may I ask?'

'Does there have to be a reason?' she countered. 'I just think that it's time. I cannot leave things to my assistant indefinitely.'

'And here was I, thinking he was Mr Perfect,' he snorted. 'Actually I think there's more to it. Yesterday you were as happy as I've ever seen you, then all of a sudden you developed an apparent fever, which I now presume was not illness at all but anger. What happened? Was it something I did? Said?'

Kirstie shook her head, not willing to tell him about Simona's sniping comments. He would think she was jealous, which she wasn't. Lucio was welcome to her. But no way was she going to stay here and watch their distasteful relationship. 'It has nothing to do with you,' she lied. 'You're forgetting I have a business to run.'

'Have you considered Rebecca?' he asked sharply. 'Does *she* want to go?'

'I've not asked her,' Kirstie answered, 'nor do I intend to. I shall simply tell her that it's time for us to return home.'

'I hope you're not planning to take my daughter away from me altogether?' There was a sudden raw edge to his voice and more than a touch of suspicion in his eyes. His whole body was as tense as a coiled spring.

'Of course not,' she said. 'You'll still have access to her; I wouldn't be that cruel.' Though she had no intention of spending any more time with him herself, not when he had Simona the siren to satisfy his carnal urges.

'But you've flatly turned down my proposal of marriage?' Eyes as hard as bullets bored into her face.

Kirstie nodded, feeling a wriggle of unease in her stomach.

'And you're not going to tell me why?' His nostrils flared and his fingers flexed and despite her discomfort Kirstie felt oddly pleased that he was angry.

'Because it wouldn't work; it's as simple as that,' she told him bluntly.

'Why wouldn't it work?' he demanded, lifting the coffee-pot and filling her cup. 'We've proved that we're compatible.'

'In bed, maybe,' she derided, 'but not in other ways. I don't want a husband who works virtually twenty-four hours a day seven days a week. I want a nine-to-five man; I've told you that before. I want someone dependable, who'll be there for his daughter.' And his wife, she could have added, but she didn't; she didn't want to ignite any more fires.

But when he started to say something in his own defence she added quickly, 'I know you're around now but only because you want to get to know Becky. Already work's pulling you. Any day now you'll be back in full swing. It's best we go while Becky still has a good impression.'

Lucio leaned back in his chair and surveyed her, his dark eyes searching. His very stillness made her afraid, made her wonder what was coming next. 'This is a very sudden decision,' he said. 'I thought we'd decided that you'd stay for the whole summer?'

'Maybe that's the impression you gained,' she retorted, her chin high, her eyes as bright as his. 'I don't remember making any promises. We've been here long enough.'

'You mean *you've* been here long enough,' he snarled, his fingers strumming on the table as he fought for control. 'I'm sorry you feel that way. I really did think that—'

'Because I let you into my bed didn't mean that I thought any differently of you,' cut in Kirstie hotly. 'It was just sex, nothing more. And now I've had my fun I want to go.'

She saw the fury erupt, the dull flush of colour in his cheeks, the darkening of his eyes, and she clutched the edge of her seat, bracing herself for a furious attack.

'You're going to be sorry you ever said that, Kirstie,' he snarled, springing to his feet and glaring down at her. 'Sorrier than you can ever imagine.' And with that he bounced out of the room.

For several long seconds Kirstie held her breath. It would be such a relief to get away from here, from him; she would be glad when she'd got him out of her hair. He did nothing but disrupt her emotions. It was something she could well do without.

Lucio would never be a one-woman man. He worked hard and played hard; probably thought it was what he deserved. Well, this was one woman who wasn't going to play his game, not any longer. As soon as she could arrange a flight she was out of here, whether Becky liked it or not.

She finished her coffee and went up to her room but when she picked up the phone it was dead. She frowned and wondered whether Lucio had something to do with it. She marched down the corridor to his bedroom but he wasn't there, then she headed downstairs to his study but he was not there either.

In the kitchen she found Marietta. 'Where's Lucio?' she asked without preamble.

The housekeeper pulled a wry face. 'He stormed out about ten minutes ago. He didn't say where he was going but he looked in one hell of a mood.'

'Why isn't my phone working?'

Marietta frowned. 'I do not know.' She picked up the kitchen phone and shook her head. 'I will get someone to look into it.'

It was late when Becky awoke and they spent the day by the pool. There was nothing left to remind them of the party; everything was back to normal. An army of people had arrived earlier and cleared the lot.

'Wasn't it a lovely party?' asked Becky, floating on her back, looking up at her mother, who sat with her feet dangling in the water.

Kirstie nodded. 'I'm glad you enjoyed it.'

'I've made lots of new friends and had loads of invitations.'

Her heart took a nosedive. 'I'm sorry, Becky, but we won't be here that long. I'm making arrangements to go home.'

'What?' Her daughter pushed to her feet and stared disbelievingly at her mother. 'Why? I thought we were staying the whole holiday? What's happened, Mum, to make you change your mind?'

'Nothing; I'm just worried about my business. I've never left—'

'I don't believe you,' declared Becky in a sudden rage. 'It's my father, isn't it? You've fallen out with him again. What's the matter with you two? It's perfectly clear you love each other and yet you keep arguing.'

'I do not love your father,' declared Kirstie firmly. 'He's—'

'He's what? He's good and kind and caring, and even if you go back to England I'm not. I'm having the time of my life here—you can't make me come.'

Kirstie closed her eyes. She had been afraid of this. 'You have no choice, Becky,' she said determinedly. 'We're both leaving and that's that.'

'What does Dad say?'

Kirstie drew in a deep breath.

'You haven't told him, have you? You're going to run away and let him find out afterwards. Where is he now? I want to speak to him.'

'Your father's out,' said Kirstie.

'Then I'll ring him.'

'The phones aren't working.'

'I hate you, Mum.'

Kirstie felt as though a knife had been stabbed into her heart. She had never thought she would hear her daughter say these words. 'You'll see your father again, darling. I'm not forbidding you seeing him. I just think we've holidayed long enough. He's anxious to get back to work too, you know.'

Becky's shoulders slumped and she turned away and swam slowly across the pool. For the rest of the day she was moodily silent.

It was almost nine o'clock when Lucio came home. He looked tired and drawn but Kirstie felt no compassion. 'What have you done to the phone?' she asked abruptly.

'What have *I* done?'

'It's not working.'

'I'll get on to it.'

'Marietta promised to do that but nothing's happened.'

'Who did you want to ring?'

'The airport,' she snapped.

'So you haven't changed your mind?'

'No.'

'And Rebecca?'

Kirstie shrugged.

'She's not happy about it, is she?' he asked sharply. 'And I can't say I blame her. Lord knows what sort of foolish notion you have in your mind but you shouldn't let our daughter suffer because of it.' He paused and seemed to be thinking hard. 'If you still insist on going, why don't you leave her here with me? I'll bring her back at the end of the holiday.'

'I can't do that,' said Kirstie, the very thought horrifying her.

'Why not?' he asked crisply.

'Because I've never left her anywhere.' Apart from the odd sleepover at her friend's.

'Then it's about time you did. She's a big girl now. She's almost a woman. And you know she'll be perfectly safe here.'

Kirstie wondered whether she dared. Becky would be over the moon, she knew that, but could she trust Lucio to keep his word? 'You're planning on staying here in Barcelona for the rest of the summer?'

He nodded, watching her closely from beneath lowered lids. She could see nothing of his eyes but she could feel their power nevertheless. Could she trust him? 'I'll see what Becky says,' she said faintly.

Lucio instantly smiled. A wide smile that lit up his face and took the tiredness out of it. 'Let's find her now.'

'She's in her room.'

Together they went up and Becky looked at them warily. Dried tears stained her cheeks and her eyes were red-rimmed. Kirstie instantly ran over and took her into her arms. The decision was made for her. 'Your father says that if you want to stay it's all right with him.'

Becky looked at Lucio over her mother's shoulder. 'I can, Dad?'

He nodded.

'Oh, thank you. Thank you both, and I'm sorry, Mum, for saying I hated you earlier. I don't really. I was upset.'

'I know, sweetheart.' Kirstie hugged her daughter tightly and then let her go, and Becky ran over to her father and gave him a hug too. Kirstie hoped she wasn't making a big mistake. 'Your father's promised to bring you back in time for your return to school. You make sure that he does.'

'I will.'

When Kirstie finally went to bed all she could see in her mind's eye was Lucio's triumphant smile.

Three days later she returned home alone.

CHAPTER FIFTEEN

'I CAN'T understand this,' said Kirstie, looking through her order records for what had to be the hundredth time.

She had thought that she could safely leave her affairs in Jonathon's hands but something had gone drastically wrong. She had been home several days now and she'd gone over and over the figures until her head spun. None of it made sense.

Sales were down and orders had been cancelled. 'What's going on?' she demanded of him.

Jonathon lifted his shoulders in a worried shrug. 'Believe me, if I knew I would tell you. I'm as concerned as you.' He was a slim-built man in his early thirties with mousy brown hair and a timid expression. But he was a wizard with figures and had an excellent telephone manner. He knew her business inside out and if anyone could make a go of it in her absence he could.

So what had happened?

'Have you contacted these people and asked them why they've cancelled orders?'

'I have,' he said. 'All I got was some sort of noncommittal response. No one's prepared to talk.'

Kirstie's brows dragged together and her heart pumped uneasily. This was her living; she couldn't afford to lose business like this. She was OK for the moment, but if sales continued to slump, where would it leave her? With a huge mortgage to pay, a daughter to put through university and no means of funding either of them, that was where.

She dropped her head in her hands, feeling ill. Coming on top of her last three uneasy days in Barcelona, when Lucio had made her life distinctly unpleasant by constantly questioning her decision, she felt like drowning her sorrows in drink.

'There has to be an answer,' she said, wondering if Jonathon himself was to blame. She had thought she could trust him, but… She let her thoughts fade away. Jonathon had been with her for years; he was an old friend. He wouldn't do anything to jeopardise her business, she felt sure.

Unless he'd enjoyed running her business while she was away and had notions of starting up for himself? Pull the rug from under her feet and then fill the gap in the market! A cold shiver ran down her spine. Surely not!

'Are there faults in our programmes?' she asked. 'Have we had any complaints? Have you checked them recently?'

'I've done everything I can think of,' he answered.

'But you never thought to ring me in Spain and tell me what was going on?'

'I didn't want to worry you; I thought I could handle things, I thought I'd be able to find out what was wrong.'

Kirstie had no choice but to believe him but she decided to make a few phone calls herself. She still came up with nothing. People with whom she'd had a close relationship over the years were not prepared to talk.

And with each passing week her finances zeroed lower and lower until in the end she knew that she would have to sell up. Probably sell the house as well.

Whenever Becky phoned she put on her most cheerful

voice, telling her how much she loved her and missed her and couldn't wait for her to come home. She didn't ask about Lucio and he never volunteered to speak to her, for which she was thankful. She could just imagine how he would gloat if he ever found out that her company was failing.

He'd probably offer to buy it at a knockdown price, or at least he'd want copyright on her software programmes. Not that they'd do him much good these days when sales were down to almost single figures.

Kirstie hardly slept at night and she felt ill with worry. Occasionally she let herself think about Lucio and their fantastic lovemaking, and her body would grow warm and she would wonder whether she had made a mistake, but then would come a vision of the lady in red and she would know that she hadn't.

By the end of the summer her finances were such that she closed down the business and put her house on the market. She dreaded telling Becky that they would be moving to a smaller house, guessing that her daughter would suggest they move in with Lucio permanently. But she didn't want his pity; there was no way she could handle that.

On the day Becky was due home she polished the house from top to bottom and put on her brightest face. She prayed that Lucio's driver would bring her daughter from the airport and not Lucio himself.

Her prayers were not answered.

When she saw him unfold himself from the car her spirits fell. But when she saw Becky jump out she forgot about Lucio and welcomed her daughter with open arms. 'I've missed you so much.'

'I've missed you too, Mum. What's with the For Sale sign?'

Kirstie cursed her own stupidity in forgetting all about the board planted in their front garden.

'Not thinking of running away, are we?' asked Lucio softly, his sepia eyes cuttingly sharp on hers. He wore a grey silk suit and white shirt and he looked dangerously attractive. All the feelings she had jammed tightly out of the way came surging back.

'Why would I want to do that?' she asked defensively, hating herself for being so weak.

Broad shoulders lifted. 'You tell me.'

They were in the house by this time and he followed her into the lounge. I'm not running, I'm being forced, she felt like saying, but she didn't want Lucio to know what had happened since her return, for she knew as sure as summer followed spring that he would gloat. And so she turned to Becky instead. 'What a wonderful tan you have.'

'You should have stayed, Mum. Dad's taken me to some fantastic places, and I've been to lots of parties. I've enjoyed myself so much.'

Not so much that she didn't want to come home, hoped Kirstie. She was surprised to hear that Lucio had been taking her out. She really had thought it would be back to business for him and Becky would have to amuse herself. 'I'm pleased you've had a good time, sweetheart.'

'And how about you?' asked Lucio, settling himself into an armchair and looking as though he was prepared to stay. 'What have you been doing with yourself? How's business, for instance? And why are you selling your house? Are you moving further upmarket? Are things that good?'

How Kirstie wished she could say that she was doing well. Instead she was a failure. And it hurt like hell. 'I'm OK,' she said.

'Just that? OK?'

'I'm going to my room, Mum,' interrupted Becky.

'I'll carry your stuff up,' said Lucio, springing to his feet.

Kirstie was glad of a few minutes to herself. She needed

time to decide how much she should tell Lucio. The truth, or a lie? A half-truth perhaps? Or nothing at all? It was actually none of his business.

'So, suppose you tell me what's wrong?' He was back with her, relaxed in his chair, one leg crossed over the other, his eyes ever watchful on her face.

He looked so concerned, so *caring,* that Kirstie felt her iron will crumble. 'I've lost my business.' Her voice cracked and tears stung the backs of her eyes.

Lucio frowned and sat up straight. 'Tell me about it.'

Through her tears Kirstie managed to describe the sequence of events that had happened since her return.

'And this is why you're selling your house?'

'I simply can't afford it any more,' she said.

'Then you must move in with me,' he said at once. And when Kirstie began to protest he added, 'It's the only answer. My home here is big enough to house a dozen families. You can have your own suite of rooms; we can live independent lives if you wish. But at least I'll be able to see my daughter on a regular basis, and that can only be good for her. What do you think?'

'I feel,' said Kirstie slowly, 'as though I've been driven into a corner. I feel as though I'm being given no choice.'

'Would it be so bad?' he asked gently.

'I guess not.' Becky would be in her element and at least Simona wouldn't be here.

Although there was no saying that he didn't have other girlfriends. She'd seen enough photographs of him in the glossies to know that he didn't lead a celibate life.

'So you'll move in?'

Was that a jubilant gleam in his eyes or was she imagining things? She could do worse. She could move into a tiny house that she and Becky would both hate. 'I'll give it a try,' she said. 'I already have a purchaser so if the sale goes through I'll move in with you on a temporary basis. If we're happy there, I'll stay. If not, I'll carry on with my plans of buying something smaller.'

'It's a deal.' He stood up and held out his hand and this time Kirstie definitely saw an exultant flash in his devilishly dark eyes. Her downfall was his prize, she thought as she took his hand.

'I'll make sure you don't regret this,' he said, 'and Becky's going to love it. She said only this morning that she was going to miss me. But at least I won't be going over to Spain for a little while, so she can see as much of me as she likes.'

When he had gone Kirstie began to wonder whether she had done the right thing. Becky was over the moon, as they had both known she would be, but Kirstie had several reservations. Not least of which was whether Lucio was planning a concerted attack on her defences.

When she had put her hand into his she had felt an instant sizzle of awareness. She had forgotten how strong the attraction between them was. What would it be like living under the same roof? Would she inevitably end up in his bed or would he honour her wishes and let them lead their separate lives?

During the next few weeks while her sale was going through Kirstie lived in a state of apprehension. While her daughter danced around in high anticipation Kirstie felt as though she was making a huge mistake.

Lucio was a frequent visitor and he made all the arrangements for storing her furniture and anything else she didn't want to take with her. On the day of the move he was outside his house, waiting to greet them.

'Welcome to my home,' he said with the widest of smiles, 'and I hope you will make it yours.'

It was a bit too much like a stately home for Kirstie to feel that, but the rooms he had chosen for them on the first floor had been newly decorated and were not so intimidating as the main reception rooms. The colours were subtle, the furniture modern, and Becky had given a whoop of sheer joy. Especially when she discovered a brand-new state-of-the-art computer system in her room.

'You're the best dad ever,' she claimed, flinging her arms round his neck.

Lucio smiled triumphantly and Kirstie wondered in what other ways he was going to spoil his daughter. She would need to have a word with him—yet again!

During the days that followed Lucio left them strictly alone; in fact he never seemed to be at home, and, although Becky grumbled, as far as Kirstie was concerned it was the perfect solution.

'This is what your dad's like,' she said when Becky complained that she rarely saw him. 'Work is his god.'

'Well, I'm not going to stand for it,' declared Becky. 'I'm going to tell him. We're here as a family now; he should be with us.'

Kirstie shook her head. 'I don't think that's quite what we are. Your father has kindly given us a roof over our heads, but we're not living together in the true sense of the words. I'll have a word with him if you like.'

Becky nodded and as if the gods had played into their hands Lucio came home early from work and they all sat down for dinner together in the downstairs dining room.

'Dad, why are you always out?' asked Becky before Kirstie could say anything, a truculent expression on her face. 'I've hardly seen you since we moved in.'

Kirstie shot her a warning look. She knew what her daughter was like when she got a bee in her bonnet.

But Lucio did not take offence. 'I'm a very busy man, my darling. I also thought that you'd need time to settle in.'

'Well, we're settled,' said Becky, 'and I want to spend some quality time with my father. Is it too much to ask?'

She was far less diplomatic than Kirstie would have been, but she seemed to be doing OK. Lucio smiled at his daughter indulgently. 'Then that's what you shall have.'

Later, after Becky had gone up to her room to finish her homework, Lucio asked Kirstie if she would join him for a drink. 'I'm sure you must be lonely, sitting up in your room night after night while Becky does her homework.'

'It's no different from when I was at home,' she answered with a vague shrug. 'I sometimes walk in the gardens. They're very beautiful, Lucio. A credit to you.'

'Except that I don't do all the hard work,' he acknowledged with a surprisingly sheepish grin.

No, he didn't do anything except dream up new ways to make money, thought Kirstie.

'Would you like to walk out there now? It's a beautiful balmy night.'

Kirstie hesitated for only a few seconds. 'Yes, I think I'd like that.' September this year was warm and golden with summer-like temperatures. Some of the leaves were beginning to turn but it looked as though autumn would be late in arriving.

But as they strolled down the sloping lawn and headed for the copse Kirstie began to wish that she hadn't been so keen. Walking at his side, bodies not quite touching but close enough for her to feel the male essence of him, made her realise that she was still very much attracted to him, and could be in grave danger of giving herself away.

'Are you settled in here now?'

'Yes, thank you.'

'Is there anything that you need?'

'No, you've thought of everything.'

'Does Rebecca need anything?'

'No.'

'What do you do with yourself all day?'

Mundane conversation that she had no wish to indulge in! Why did he care? He was away so much that she could sit and brood and he wouldn't know. In fact she was trying to find herself a job. The money from the sale of her house sat in the bank gaining interest; she was not going to touch that in case it didn't work out here. Meanwhile, though, she did not want to sponge off Lucio.

'Do you really care?'

Lucio frowned. 'Of course I do. I don't want you to be bored.'

'Since you've given your cook instructions to provide our meals, and since your maid cleans our rooms and does our laundry, there's not much else for me to do other than be bored, is there?' she asked crossly.

He looked surprised by her outburst. 'I thought it would help.'

'Help be damned,' she cried. 'You have no idea, do you? I'm already beginning to think that it was a big mistake accepting your hospitality. I might start to look around for a place of our own.'

'Is Rebecca unhappy too?' His face was dark now with a mixture of anger and puzzlement.

'No, she loves it. Her only grumble is that you're never here.'

'I didn't think you'd want me hanging around.'

'I'm not talking about me,' she retorted crisply. 'Your daughter loves you dearly and she's feeling hurt by this sudden withdrawal.'

'The same as I felt hurt when you decided to rush back here,' he countered.

'You know why I did that,' she riposted. 'And I'm glad I did because look what happened. If I'd waited any longer I'd have been in dire trouble. At least all my bills are paid and I haven't ended up in debt.' Though it was small consolation after all the hard work she'd put in.

'You could work for me.'

Kirstie lifted her brows. 'I don't need any more of your charity.'

He looked affronted by her statement but he didn't comment on it, saying instead, 'You're very good at your job. We could do with people like you.'

'No, thank you! If I want a job I'll find one for myself. And I couldn't be that good if my sales started dropping. I guess I got too complacent. I should never have left Jonathon in charge.'

'Do you blame him?'

'Who else is there?' she asked with a sharp glance in his direction. And then she wished she hadn't looked at him because what she saw in his eyes was hot desire. Gone in an instant but there all the same.

She hurried a few steps ahead. They were in the forest now, a peaceful place that she loved. It was cool during the day and still pleasant now. The tracery of branches blocked out most of the evening sky but it was still light enough to see where they were walking.

Except that Kirstie's thoughts were on Lucio and not where she was going. Just that very brief glimpse of his feelings had undone her tightly suppressed emotions. Her whole body zinged with renewed energy and her stomach muscles clenched as she tried to quell a rising need. This wasn't supposed to be happening. She must not give in to these dangerous feelings that were rising like a flood tide, welling and threatening to break at any minute.

But in her haste to put space between them Kirstie caught her toe on a fallen branch and, unable to help herself, she pitched forward and fell heavily to the floor.

Lucio was immediately at her side, full of concern. 'Kirstie, are you all right? Have you hurt yourself?'

'I don't think so.' She felt shaken but not hurt and she stretched her limbs experimentally.

'Let me help you up.'

'No, I'm all right; I can manage,' she said fiercely. She didn't want him touching her. She didn't want that male body anywhere near.

'Nonsense.' He was down on his knees beside her, his hands reaching out.

Kirstie saw what was coming but it was too late to avoid him. He took her arms and helped her into a sitting position and then, his eyes midnight dark, a groan of sheer agony escaping the back of his throat, he kissed her.

A tender kiss to start with but when he felt no resistance his kiss deepened, his tongue touching and tasting hers, probing, arousing, demanding. Senses awoke with a burst and Kirstie was soon lost in a world where nothing else mattered. The kiss was deep and searching and utterly mind-blowing.

When he laid her back down on the soft forest floor the full length of him followed, and when his exploring fingers touched her cheeks, her eyelids, her nose, and finally her mouth, Kirstie was breathless with need of him. She sucked a finger into her mouth and he moaned and replaced it with his searching tongue. His eyes were black with desire, his body hot, and when his hands began an exploration of their own Kirstie gave herself up to the inevitable.

Kiss followed kiss followed kiss, hot and hungry, provoking tingling sensations she had never felt before, flowing up through her bloodstream like dancing molten metal, while his fingers drew further unbelievable sensations from her breasts. He knew exactly how much pressure to exert on her nipples to have her writhing and wriggling beneath him. He knew how far to go, when to stop and give her breathing space, and when to start his assault on her senses again.

When his hand slid beneath her full cotton skirt and skilful fingers found the hot core of her desire she cried out. 'Lucio, what are you doing to me?'

'You want me to stop?' He paused temporarily, dark eyes both searching and damning. He knew what he wanted and he was going to take it, and goodness help her; she hadn't the will-power to stop him.

'No!' It was a tiny no, a pained no. It hurt her to admit it, but he had gone too far now, he had awoken her sleeping feelings and they demanded nothing less than full satisfaction.

'But maybe here isn't the place,' he said gruffly. 'I think somewhere more comfortable. Like my bed?' His face was as suffused with heat and desire as her own, his eyes like two glowing coals that burnt right into her heart.

Kirstie didn't want him to stop now; she didn't want to let these feelings slip away. It felt good, so good; she had forgotten how expertly Lucio could arouse her every base instinct. Her body sang and she didn't want it to stop. She wanted him to finish what he had started, she wanted to feel him inside her, she wanted complete and utter fulfilment. Nothing less would do.

So in answer to his question she pulled his face down to hers again and this time it was her hand that sought and found the pulsing heat of his manhood.

Lucio groaned over and over again. 'You do know what you're doing, Kirstie?'

'Mm.' It was all she could manage. There was enough fire inside her to set the whole forest alight.

In less time than it took for her to draw much needed breath Lucio had readied himself. With another swift movement her panties were discarded and he lowered himself over her prone and expectant body.

Kirstie cried out as he entered her.

'I'm hurting you?' he asked, stilling for a moment.

'No! Never! It's exquisite. Love me, Lucio; love me like you've never loved me before.'

He needed no second bidding. Their bodies swelled and melded and fire burst in their bellies, and in all too short a space of time it was over. Lucio lay sated at her side, breathing hard, spasms still overtaking him as they did her own body too.

She lay with her eyes closed for a long, long time and when she opened them it was almost dark. Lucio was propped up on one elbow, watching her, fingers of moonlight filtering through the leafy canopy painting silver highlights on his face and shoulders.

'Are you all right, Kirstie?'

She smiled blissfully. 'I've never been more all right in my life.' And it was true, even though somewhere deep down inside her began the rumblings of guilt. She squashed them with the same merciless feeling as when swiping a fly.

'You must be uncomfortable.'

'A little.'

'Here, let me help you up.' He sprang to his feet and held out his hands. Once she was upright his arms drew her to him again, warm arms, firm arms, possessive arms. And he kissed her, not fiercely this time but gently and carefully. And then he looked deep into her eyes. 'This is as good for you as it is for me?'

'Yes,' she whispered. 'I wanted to reject you but something inside wouldn't let me.'

'I'm pleased to hear that,' he said, 'because there's something inside me that refuses to let you go.' He took her hand. 'Let's get back to the house.'

They slept together that night, and every night after that, and Lucio began coming home at a reasonable hour. Everyone was happy.

Until the day that Kirstie answered the phone and heard Simona's dulcet tones asking to speak to Lucio.

A chill crept through Kirstie's body in as much time as it took her to say, 'I'm sorry, he's not here.' She had hoped, and prayed in fact, that Lucio had finished with Simona. Not once had he mentioned her name in recent weeks so why was she phoning? Unless it was to do with business? Her heart lightened a little and then plunged low again. If that was the case, wouldn't she ring him at the office?

'Who am I speaking to?' Simona asked impatiently.

'Don't you recognise my voice, Simona? It's Kirstie.' At the other end of the line she heard a disbelieving breath.

'What are *you* doing there?' asked the other woman peevishly.

Kirstie smiled to herself; she was enjoying this. 'I live here now.'

A long silence ensued, and then Simona spat a few words that turned Kirstie's world upside down. 'I knew that your business venture had failed, but I didn't realise that you'd moved in with Lucio. What happened? Did he take pity on you?'

'How did you know about my business?' asked Kirstie sharply. 'Did Lucio tell you?' He'd had no right—it was personal and devastating and she didn't wish the whole world to know.

Simona took her time in answering and Kirstie could almost see a satisfied smirk on her face. 'How did I know? That's very simple. Lucio was the one who did the dirty deed.'

CHAPTER SIXTEEN

THE chill in Kirstie's heart turned to frozen disbelief. 'Lucio told you that he was responsible for the downfall of my company?' It was hard to believe. And if it was true it was even harder to accept that she had been so taken in by him.

'No, Lucio didn't tell me,' answered Simona, 'I found out for myself. I listened to his phone calls; I read bits of paper. I meant nothing to him when you came on the scene. He wanted you unreservedly and when you left, when you gave every appearance of not wanting to see him ever again, he dreamt up his plot. He thought that if you were poor enough and homeless you would have no choice but to turn to him. It looks like his plan worked,' she thrust disgustedly. 'Are you sleeping together? Are you a cosy little family now? Are you…?'

But Kirstie wasn't listening.

Lucio had sent her company crashing!

He had ruined her!

Everything that had happened to her was his fault!

And he had pretended to help, to care and support her, even inveigled her into his bed!

She was spitting mad and without saying another word to Simona she slammed down the phone.

When Lucio came home that evening she was ready for

him. Becky had rung to say that she was sleeping over at a friend's and Kirstie had willingly agreed. It would give her the privacy she needed to confront Lucio.

Lucio took one look at Kirstie's face and knew that something was very wrong. He had not seen her as angry since the day he refused to marry her nearly seventeen years ago.

His heart dipped into his shoes. Everything had been going along swimmingly this last week or two and he had been planning to propose. He had even bought the engagement ring. Now it looked as though she was ready to walk out on him again.

'What's the matter?' he asked, dropping his briefcase to the floor and throwing his jacket on a chair before loosening his tie and unbuttoning his collar, which felt as though it was going to strangle him. He wanted to take her into his arms and kiss her and tell her that whatever it was he would put it right. But it looked more than that. For some as yet unknown reason she was seriously mad with him.

'How could you?' she demanded. 'How could you do that to me?'

He frowned. 'What have I done?'

'You took away my business!'

His heart slammed against his ribcage. How the hell had she found out about that? He closed his eyes and let out a deep breath.

'And don't try to deny it,' she shrieked, 'because I know it's true.'

'Yes, it's true,' he admitted.

His confession seemed to take the wind out of her sails, for she stood stock still and stared at him and he had never seen her more beautiful. Her lovely amethyst eyes with their fringe of thick dark lashes were wide and incredulous, and her flushed face gave her a heightened beauty. She wore a matching amethyst top and white trousers that emphasised her slender figure, though he did think that she'd put on a bit of weight recently. Not surprising with the dishes his cook prepared. And she looked better for it.

He'd been daydreaming in his car on the way home about making love to her, something he never tired of, and which Kirstie loved too. In fact she was an insatiable lover these days and it made him realise what he'd been missing all these years.

'So why did you do it?' she demanded of him now. 'Why did you set out to ruin me?'

'Not ruin you, my darling; I—'

'Don't darling me!' she snapped. 'I am no longer your darling. I am out of here as soon as I find somewhere else to live.'

Lucio gave an inward groan. He had hoped that Kirstie would never find out because he knew what her reaction would be. She would call him all sorts of a low-down swine, and she would tell him she never wanted to see him again. He needed to be careful how he answered her. He was fighting for his life now. For his future.

'I did it for us.'

His response brought a swift and vicious frown to her normally smooth brow. 'For *us*? How do you make that out?'

'I could think of no other way to bring you back into my life.'

'You selfish bastard!' She took a lunge at him and would have slapped him across the face if he hadn't caught her wrist. 'I hate you, Lucio Masterton. I hate you with all my heart.'

'Kirstie.' He took both hands then and imprisoned them. 'Hear me out. Listen to what I have to say.'

'It will make no difference,' she stormed, her eyes spitting bullets at him.

Lord, she was magnificent. He wanted to kiss her instead of argue. He wanted to hold her against him and quell her shaking body. Most of all he wanted to make love to her. He could easily make her forget her anger; he could take her away from all of this into another world of spiralling sensations and throbbing desire.

'Kirstie, I love you.'

She stopped struggling and stared at him in open-mouthed disbelief. 'You love me? And yet you've ruined me! What sort of crazy logic is that?'

'I love you and I want you to be my wife. You ran away from me in Spain because you couldn't keep away from your business any longer. I couldn't compete with that. I had to find a way round it.'

'So you destroyed my business! You know what I think, Lucio? I think that the only reason you want to marry me is for Rebecca's sake. I don't think love has anything to do with it. We have good sex together, I admit that, but that's as far as it goes, and it's certainly not a basis for marriage.'

'You're wrong, Kirstie. Very wrong! I love you with everything I have. I was a fool to ever let you go.'

'And I was a fool to let you back into my bed. But no more, Lucio! No more! This is most definitely the end.'

He felt his gut twist into knots and his brain searched desperately for some other way to convince her that he was telling the truth. He came up with nothing. In any case Kirstie was in no mood to listen. 'Tell me,' he said, 'how did you find out?'

Her laugh was bitter and dry and held no amusement. 'From a very good friend of yours! At least, she was. I wonder if you'll want to speak to her again after this?'

Lucio frowned. What friend? No one knew what he'd done; he'd made sure of that.

'I'll tell you, shall I?' she asked, wicked delight in her voice. 'Or maybe I'll give you three guesses.'

'Quit the stalling,' he snarled. His nerves were on the verge of snapping. He couldn't take much more of this. Today, he had reckoned, was his last chance. If Kirstie said no to his marriage proposal he wouldn't ask her again. But everything had gone dramatically wrong and he was fighting now for the woman he loved.

'It was Simona,' she informed him coolly. 'Your dear friend Simona! The woman of unrequited love.'

'Simona?' he queried, dark eyes full of shocked disbelief.

'The very same.'

'She phoned you?'

'She phoned *you*. But you weren't here and I was and she was, to put it mildly, extremely surprised. Or maybe horrified would be a better word. She didn't like the thought that I was living with you, so she imparted that little piece of juicy information in the belief that it would send me running. And do you know what, Lucio? She was right.'

Lucio felt himself reeling. 'How did she know? I never told her.'

'She spied on you, it's as simple as that. She was jealous of your attention to me. I know you're not aware of it but we had quite a little discussion about it at Becky's party.'

'You did?' Was there to be no end to the shocks she was giving him?

'She told me all about her being your *very personal* assistant. She told me that she was in love with you and that you'd been planning to get married before I put in an appearance. She was very upset. It's no wonder she felt disgruntled enough to pry into your private affairs.'

'She's a liar,' stormed Lucio in disbelief. He found it hard to believe it of Simona, but he had no reason to believe that Kirstie was lying. As a matter of fact he would take Kirstie's word against Simona's any day.

'Do you deny that you took her to bed on the day of Becky's party?'

'I did what?' he gasped. 'She told you that?'

'Simona didn't have to tell me anything. I saw for myself what happened. You disappeared into the house and when you next appeared Simona was straightening her clothes. She looked like the cat who'd got the cream.'

'Dammit, Kirstie, all we were doing was talking business.'

'And I'm expected to believe that, am I?' she rasped.

'Simona was, is in love with me, I won't deny that,' he said on a deep sigh. 'Or at least she thinks she is. She's chased me for years. I've taken it all in good part. I even let her persuade me to give her a temporary job as my PA while Maria was away on maternity leave. She's back now so Simona is at a loose end again. She doesn't need to work—her father's very wealthy; she—'

'She did it to be close to you,' snapped Kirstie. 'According to her you've been very generous to her as well.'

Lucio shrugged. 'I may have bought her a trinket or two.'

'Or paid for her to go on holiday?'

He frowned and Kirstie nodded.

'It's another lie,' he declared strongly. 'I didn't want her to go, not while Maria was away and I was in England, but she insisted it was already booked.'

'And you're such a soft touch where a pretty woman's concerned. Spare me the sob story, Lucio. You bring it all on yourself.'

He felt that he was getting nowhere and stalked across to his drinks cupboard and poured himself a whisky, which he downed in one swallow before refilling his glass. 'Do you want a drink?' he asked belatedly.

Kirstie shook her head.

'Was Simona the real reason you left?' he asked. 'You thought I was in love with her?' If so, perhaps he stood a chance. He certainly wasn't going to give Kirstie up without a fight. One way or another he needed to persuade her that he really did love her and that he wanted to marry her. Perhaps if he produced the ring it might help? But he decided against it. He needed to get her on side first.

'Yes,' she admitted in a much quieter tone than she'd been using. In fact she looked drained. He had never seen her so pale.

'Why don't you sit down?' he asked gently.

She did as he asked and he sat too, facing her, watching her, wishing all over again that he'd not been such a fool. Many years ago his father had told him in no uncertain terms that he was making a big mistake but he hadn't listened.

While his mother had been glad. She admired her son's ambition and didn't think he should let any woman stand in his way. In fact she'd never liked Kirstie, even though Kirstie had never done anything to upset her. He wondered why, and he wondered what his mother would say now if she could see him practically begging Kirstie to marry him.

He took another swallow of his drink. 'Now that we have it all out in the open, Kirstie, will you reconsider? I love you dearly and I'm deeply, deeply sorry for everything I've done. I was desperate and it seemed like the only way to have you all to myself. I will never hurt you again as long as I live, I promise. I will love you and cherish you for ever.'

He watched her face, saw the emotions chasing over it;

fury, sadness, regret and finally a faint smile. 'I think I may have a drink after all.'

It wasn't exactly the answer he'd been hoping for but he got up and poured her a gin and tonic, which he knew was her favourite, handing it to her, aching to pull her up into his arms but resuming his seat again. He would give her as much time as she needed if he thought the answer would ultimately be yes.

Daringly he plucked the small leather box from his pocket and took out the ring, twisting it in his fingers so that she could see the glitter of the biggest diamond he had been able to find. 'This is for you, my darling. Just say the word and—'

Slowly, Kirstie rose to her feet, placing her glass down in the process, and walked over to him. 'Oh, Lucio! What have we done to each other? I can't put myself through this torture any longer.'

'Torture?' he queried.

'Surely you know that I love you too? I always have, even if I've told myself I don't. You've hurt me a lot, more than you'll ever know, but I understand why you did it.'

'And can you forgive me?' Lucio added, with concern in his eyes.

'Can you forgive me for keeping Becky from you for so long?' Kirstie questioned back.

Lucio sighed and ran a long finger down Kirstie's cheek. 'It seems we have both acted unfairly towards each other, doesn't it? What if we agree to a fresh beginning from now on? I love you, Kirstie. Will you marry me?'

Kirstie looked hard for a moment at the man in front of her. Slowly a smile spread across her face. 'Yes, Lucio, I will.'

She dropped onto his lap and put her arms around his neck and kissed him.

* * *

The ring was stunningly gorgeous, thought Kirstie as she waggled her fingers while looking at the light glinting off its various facets. 'You must love me an awful lot to spend so much money on me,' she said.

'More than life itself,' he declared, 'and you're worth every penny.'

When they went to bed that night their lovemaking exceeded everything that had gone before, and the very next day they began making plans for their wedding. It was going to be a large affair with about four hundred guests and they hired a wedding planner to take care of all the details.

On the day Kirstie looked spectacularly beautiful in a white silk off-the-shoulder dress embroidered with pearls and diamonds, with a train several feet long and a headdress that made her look like a princess.

She had eyes for no one except Lucio, and both of them marvelled that at last they had come together for richer for poorer, in sickness and in health, until death parted them. 'I love you,' she said to him as they walked back down the aisle as man and wife.

'And I love you with all my heart,' Lucio told her.

Becky looked stunning too in an amethyst dress and a pearl tiara, but it was her smile that shone out, dazzling everyone who looked at her. In fact she hadn't stopped smiling since Kirstie told her that she and Lucio were getting married.

The paparazzi were outside; cameras flashed, videos whirred. They were going to be all over the papers tomorrow and on the television too. But Kirstie did not care. She was finally united to the man she loved. Her life would be different but with Lucio at her side she could handle anything.

Lucio's parents and many other members of his family

had flown over for the wedding and his mother came up to her during the wedding reception held in a giant marquee in the mansion grounds, and she took hold of Kirstie's hands. 'Kirstie, I want to apologise for my son.'

Kirstie frowned.

'I have just heard what he did to you; in fact, he told me himself. He should never have ruined your little business. I am ashamed of him. I know he did out of a misguided sense of love, but it was the wrong way to go about it. And I have misjudged you too, Kirstie. I thought you were not good enough for my son. I was very wrong. You are all I could ever wish for in a daughter-in-law, and I hope you accept my sincerest apologies for the way I have treated you.'

This was a big admission for his mother to make and it brought tears to Kirstie's eyes. 'I accept wholeheartedly,' she said. 'You were simply being a caring mother, the same as I am towards Becky. I've no doubt I'll vet her boyfriends the same as you did me.'

This time it was the turn of the older woman's eyes to water. 'Thank you. Thank you, Kirstie. I wish you and Lucio all the happiness in the world.'

And George too came up to congratulate her. 'At last, you are part of the family.'

Later that evening Lucio surprised her by saying that he was whisking her away on honeymoon.

'I didn't know,' she breathed. 'You've already given me a wedding that's every girl's dream. I don't need to go away. I'm happy here with you.'

But he insisted and so they flew in his private jet to the south of France and here, without any interruptions, they made love all day long and all night long. Sometimes they stopped for food, or to take a walk barefooted along the sand. But if anyone had asked her where paradise was, Kirstie would have said that it was here. She had never been happier in her life.

And then one morning she woke with pains in her stomach and a debilitating sickness.

'Food poisoning,' said Lucio at once. 'Those oysters you had last night.' And he whisked her to a private hospital.

'We'll have you right in no time at all,' said the doctor, 'and the good news is that it's done no harm to your baby.'

'My baby?' queried Kirstie in astonishment. 'Are you telling me that I'm pregnant?' And she looked at Lucio, who had gone so pale she thought he might need one of the beds here too.

'You did not know?'

'No,' she answered huskily. 'I've missed my periods, yes, but I put it down to stress. A lot's happened in my life recently.'

'Well, Mrs Masterton,' smiled the doctor, 'let me be the first to congratulate you and tell you that you are approximately three months pregnant.'

Kirstie looked again at Lucio and he was smiling now, the colour returning to his cheeks.

He strode across to her and gathered her into his arms. 'History repeats itself, my darling. Except that this time I'm going to make sure that I play a big part in my son's upbringing.'

'Son?' she asked, her eyes twinkling.

'Son or daughter, I don't mind,' he said. 'And if he or she grows up to be as well-adjusted and happy as Rebecca then I won't have a care in the world. Did you really not know that you were pregnant?'

Kirstie shook her head, noticing out of the corner of her eye the doctor leaving the room. 'It must have happened that time up the mountain when we made love behind the waterfall. What a brilliant place to conceive. I'll remember it for ever more.'

'I love you, Mrs Masterton.'

'And I you, Lucio. We've gone through so much that our love must be all the stronger because of it.'

Lucio nodded. 'I second that.' And then he kissed her and Kirstie knew that she finally had a lifetime's happiness in front of her.